Internal CHAOS

Internal CHAOS

Battles of the Heart

KELLIE LANE

TATE PUBLISHING
AND ENTERPRISES, LLC

Scriptures taken from NKJV, KJV, NLT, and ESV versions of the Holy Bible.

The opinions expressed by the author are not necessarily those of Tate Publishing, LLC.

Published by Tate Publishing & Enterprises, LLC
127 E. Trade Center Terrace | Mustang, Oklahoma 73064 USA
1.888.361.9473 | www.tatepublishing.com

Tate Publishing is committed to excellence in the publishing industry. The company reflects the philosophy established by the founders, based on Psalm 68:11,
"The Lord gave the word and great was the company of those who published it."

Cover design by Jim Villaflores
Interior design by Caypeeline Casas

Published in the United States of America

ISBN: 978-1-63418-104-4
1. Self-Help / Abuse
2. Self-Help / Personal Growth / General
14.11.04

cha·os /ˈkāˌäs/

1. A condition or place of great disorder or confusion.
2. Behavior so unpredictable as to appear random

This book is dedicated to God's daughters all over the world who have fallen prey to spiritual manipulation and domestic misuse. You are so very precious in the eyesight of God. He loves you more than any partner ever could. Be strong and of good cheer. Your best days begin right now.

ACKNOWLEDGMENTS

I must first acknowledge Almighty God. Lord, thank you for allowing me to live to tell my story. This book is a result of my obedience to your Holy Spirit.

I would like to thank my husband Lavon for loving me and being my biggest supporter. Your presence in my life confirms that real God-fearing men still exist. At one point, I thought that my story was over. I was convinced that misery was my portion. But God! He sent you to me!

I would like to express my love to my children: Chrystian, Kailey, Khloe, Micah, Lakyn, and Lathyn. I pray that my sacrifices will charge you to do more and become more than Mommy will ever be.

Special thanks to my sister in Christ, Ms. Timiko Ilion. This book could not have been done without your expertise and insight. May God continuously bless you and Tristen.

I thank the Word of Life Church family. Pastor Joel, your powerful messages have truly inspired me. I thank you for reminding me of the importance of having a vision and seeing to it that it comes to pass.

I thank the Nu Vision Worship Center International family. Prophetess Richardson, thank you for the pearls of wisdom that you have so freely given me. Pastor Richardson, thank you for all that you've done for my family.

Many thanks to all of the sisters who shared their testimonies with the world through this writing. I know that it was difficult for you. Yet you yielded to the unction of the Holy Spirit. Although your true identities have been masked in the reading, God knows you by name and is well pleased. You were born to overcome.

Lastly, I will never write a book without acknowledging my hero, Chiquita Marie. Mama, you taught me so much. Keep watching over me from heaven.

CONTENTS

FOREWORD

Praise God for exposing the internal chaos. It is my prayer that as you journey through the pages of this anointed work; the spirit of the Lord will expose the secrets and strongholds that the enemy may have on your life.

This book provides you with real-life testimonies and experiences to help you overcome the wiles of the enemy. It provides insight into the challenges particularly faced by women all over the world: relationship issues, family curses, the healthy heart vs. the unhealthy heart, being out of control vs. quality control, as well how to experience growth and maturity that leads to a healthier lifestyle.

Congratulations to Kellie for allowing God to use her in this hour as she speaks truth to this generation and the generations to come.

May God richly bless every reader with a receiving heart.

Pastor Gwendolyn Richardson
Nu Vision Worship Center International
Jackson, MS

INTRODUCTION

> The Spirit of the Lord God is upon me; because the Lord hath anointed me to preach good tidings unto the meek; he hath sent me to bind up the broken-hearted, to proclaim liberty to the captives, and the opening of the prison to them that are bound.
>
> (Isaiah 61:1, KJV)

You are not reading this book for entertainment. Nor are you reading for informational use only. You are reading so that you may recognize the deceptive forces hidden behind the men who claim to love you. You are reading so that you may know how to break free from relational strongholds and demonic entrapments. By the time you reach the last page, you will understand why in times past you've made poor choices even when you had the best intentions in selecting a mate. Please expect total transformation.

> Incredible change happens in your life when you decide to take control of what you do have power over instead of craving control over what you don't.
>
> —Steve Maraboli

If you are really tired…tired of looking for love in all of the wrong places… tired of sleeping with the enemy…tired of crying…tired of the empty promises…tired of hoping…

tired of waiting for a change that may never come...tired of being in emotional, physical, and/or spiritual bondage... tired of having your heart crushed over and over again by someone you're trying desperately to love. Please know that the struggle is over. God has taken notice of you. It is your hour; it is your season. I decree it in Jesus's name.

I know what it's like to desire love and a sense of belonging above all else. I know the pain of rejection. I know how it feels to hurt so badly that you'd rather become numb to it all. For some, you've come to a place where you'd rather give up on love altogether rather than try again. For others, you can see no way out of your current situation. I've been right where many of you reading are right now. I felt hopeless. I felt humiliated. I'd failed so many times that most who knew me mocked my situation. But God. It was in this low place, a place of brokenness, that I found my true rock. He is a restorer. I told God that if he could do anything with someone who had a track record as terrible as mine, then do something with me. I agreed to tell it all if it would save another woman's soul, if it would prevent another woman's heart from shattering, if it would keep another woman of power out of the grave, and if it would deter someone else from making the same painstaking errors that I did. The reality of it all is this—not everyone makes it out of unfruitful relationships alive.

> There is a path before each person that seems right,
> but it ends in death.
>
> (Proverbs 16: 25, NLT)

I have selflessly uncovered many intimate details of my life as the chapters of this work unfold. Other sisters have also uncovered their deepest secrets throughout this text all in an effort to save you. This book is the raw truth. It was intended by God to be this way. When I first began writing, I was afraid to be explicit. I was afraid that it wouldn't be considered "godly enough." I wasn't sure of how to correctly apply biblical principles. But glory be to God for his spirit that dwells within us. I have written every word under divine influence. As you read, I ask that you take time for meditation and reflection. Allow the spirit of God to speak to your heart concerning your own life. Only you know exactly where you are, and only God can meet you in that place. Don't ignore his voice. This is not a game. Some of you have been victims of spiritual identity theft. Some have been tricked into believing that you are getting exactly what you deserve from your current relationship. Some of you are still holding on to a dream. Some of you are on the verge of a nervous breakdown. Some have been entrapped by the enemy, and he is now devising a plan to destroy your children. For some, there could very well be death in your pot. You have no idea of who you are really dealing with.

The Story of Death in the Pot

> Elisha now returned to Gilgal, and there was a famine in the land. One day as the group of prophets was seated before him, he said to his servant, "Put a large pot on the fire, and make some stew for the rest of the group." One of the young men went out into the field to gather herbs and came back with a pocketful of wild gourds. He shredded them and put them into the pot without realizing they were poisonous. Some of the stew was served to the men. But after they had eaten a bite or two they cried out,

> "Man of God, there's poison in this stew!" So they would not eat it...
>
> (2 Kings 4: 38–40 NLT)

When our eyes and ears are untrained, everything looks and sounds good including the sweet lies and trickery from the person that you're in love with. Yet the end result could very well be death and destruction. My prayer is that the eyes of your understanding will be enlightened (Ephesians 1:18).

> He that has an ear...let him hear what the spirit is saying...
>
> Revelation 2:7 (KJV)

Please go with me now on this journey of self-discovery and empowerment. You are an overcomer.

> And you will know the truth, and the truth will set you free.
>
> (John 8:32 NLT)

HEART DISEASE

> He taught me also, and said unto me, Let thine heart retain my words; keep my commandments and live.
>
> (Proverbs 4:4, KJV)

The human heart is vital for human sustenance. It was strategically designed by Jehovah God to pump life into our physical bodies. On average, the human heart beats eighty thousand to one hundred thousand times a day while pumping almost two thousand gallons of oxygen-rich blood to our cells. If the heart becomes diseased, the physical body will decline. Because of its vital role, a non-beating heart always results in demise.

The most common cause of heart disease in both men and women is narrowing of the coronary arteries, which are the blood vessels that supply blood to the heart itself. The medical term is called coronary artery disease (CAD) and progresses slowly over time. It is the major reason people have heart attacks. There are also certain heart conditions that affect women more than men including coronary microvascular disease (MVD), which is a problem that affects the heart's tiny arteries, and broken heart syndrome. Yes you read that right. There is a condition called broken heart syndrome that results from extreme *emotional stress* leading to severe but often short-term heart muscle failure.

Heart disease is responsible for one out of every four female deaths in the United States. Yet it often goes undiagnosed until the condition has worsened to the point of a heart attack or stroke. Surprisingly many forms of this often fatal condition can be prevented or treated with healthy lifestyle *choices.* The key word here is *choices.*

Granted, there are certain things in life we have no control over. For instance, you can't choose who your parents are or how tall you are. You have no control over the social class you are born into. You have no control over your nationality. You can't control heredity. If your mother had high cholesterol, you are naturally at a higher risk for developing high cholesterol, which then could potentially lead to the development of heart disease over time. If your race is African-American, American Indian, or Mexican, then yes those are all uncontrollable risk factors for the development of heart disease. But then there are also controllable risk factors such as smoking and physical inactivity. Both also increase your risk for developing heart disease but only *if* you so *choose* to pollute your body with nicotine or continue to make every excuse in the Milky Way galaxy for why you can't exercise. In other words, you can't help being black or white or purple. You can't help what Mama or Grandma may have passed down through the blood line. But, you can decide whether or not to live a life that is conditioned and disciplined. You can *choose* for the most part to become physically fit. If you have some sort of physical limitation, there are still options available to assist you in becoming the best person that you can be. For sure, you can definitely choose the granola bar over the honey bun or the baked chicken over the fried chicken. What's my point? If you want to have a healthy heart, you can make the right choices that will allow you to achieve that goal. If you choose to remain ignorant to the reality that heart disease kills, you can very well do so. God gave every human being *a free will.* You can pretty much do what you want with your life. You can live ruthless and reckless, or you can live a life that is productive and fruitful. It's totally up to you.

You may be asking what in the world does this have to do with being in a healthy, loving relationship. The commonality here is *choices*. It's all about choices. And what guides our choices? The condition of our hearts. Just as the physical heart and the choices we make affect our physical vitality, God also gave each of us a spiritual heart which plays an even more critical role.

> My flesh and my heart may fail, but God is the strength of my heart and my portion forever.
>
> (Psalm 73:26, ESV)

The spiritual heart functions in much the same way as the physical heart. It pumps life to the spirit and is the source of our inner existence. In its healthy state, the spiritual heart fears God and is empowered by the Holy Spirit. This type of heart is essentially in tune with God, and all becomes well. You will find yourself walking to the beat of the Holy Ghost. If he says move, you move. If he says go this way, you go "this way. " If he says, "No don't do that," you don't do it. It becomes just that simple. Your ears will be in tune with his voice. Your heart will actually lead you in the right direction because it's not you guiding you. The spirit of God begins to guide you. A person who is spiritually in tune with God can't help but shine above the rest. A physically fit person is easily recognized right? Yes. Well, a spiritually fit person is also easily recognized. They do not behave irrationally. They have a tendency to make sound decisions. Their relationships and social skills are on point. More than likely their physical appearance is magnetic. There's just something about this type of person that catches your eye. You may not be able to quite put your finger on it, but you know that there is something different about them. If you just so happen to spend some time around this type of person, you will then see that their lives are in order in every area, including the area of relationships. I did not say perfect; I said in order. This person allows the Holy Spirit to be the driving force behind all actions. As a result, he or she can safely discern what is good and what isn't. If single, when it comes to mate selection, this person can easily recognize a "potential" from a "no-no. " Regardless of whether the decision is to make a healthy food choice or a healthy relationship choice, the odds are in this person's favor. This type of person can enjoy life in a state of wellness and totality.

Ponder this for a moment.

If the Spirit of God, who is our chief advocate, protector, teacher, and intercessor, were in constant communication with God on one end and with you on the other, what types of choices do you think you would make? How would your life look then? What type of relationships would you have? Who would you be attracted to? Who would be attracted to you? Wouldn't you expect to gain strength in every area of your life too?

Spiritual Demise

Just as there are many diseases and disorders that can affect the physical heart, there are many ailments of the spiritual heart that can impair growth and development as a believer. If the spiritual heart becomes diseased there will be a decline in one's spiritual vitality. You will find yourself off track. Your sense of discernment will become impaired which in turn affects your decision making. When the spiritual heart becomes diseased your walk with God isn't what it used to be. You may no longer be able to hear his voice as you used to. You will find yourself with less conviction when you do things that are outside of his will. You may become so caught up in your own desires that you eventually disconnect from God altogether. You are basically "doing your own thing." You will find yourself making the same mistakes over and over again. You will lack the ability to safely decide who can and cannot enter into your life. Before you know it you've lost your focus. It's like one day you wake up and say, "How did I get here?"

We discussed risk factors for development of physical heart disease. Now let's discuss a few of the risk factors for the development of spiritual heart disease, all of which are controllable.

Bitterness and Anger

You cannot receive anything from God with bitterness and anger in your heart. Yes you've been hurt. Yes you've been lied to, but you still have to make a decision to get God's best for your life. Stop being mad at the world because he did you wrong. How can you move forward if you're still stuck in reverse? And what God-fearing man would want a woman who's frowned up and rude all of the time anyway? You've got to get rid of the "all men are dogs" syndrome. If you carry that belief in your heart and continuously speak those words from your mouth, what type of man do you expect to attract? Think about it.

> Death and life are in the power of the tongue: and they that love it shall eat the fruit thereof.
>
> (Proverbs 18:21, KJV)

Jealousy

Ladies, we must stop being jealous of one another. Jealousy is not of God. In other words, don't hate on her because she has a college degree and you don't. Go to school if you so desire. Don't become envious because she's enjoying the fruit of making the right choices. Don't hate on the next woman because she has done what it takes to be in a secure relationship with a Godly man. Did she fast, pray, and believe God for him? I know that's how I finally got my real man. That strategy works. Trust me.

Do not covet or even entertain the thought of "what if I had her man." Listen, you will never get your godly man if you're carrying what belongs to someone else in your heart. No he wouldn't treat you the way he treats her. You're not her, so stop the madness. Stop trying to look sexy around him. He is not your man. If this woman just so happens to be your friend, you should be even more ashamed. What kind of friend are you? We were not designed to compete with one another. We were created to lift one another up. We are to catch one another if we should fall…not stomp on another woman's head in our efforts to captivate the heart of her man. There have to be limits to how far one will go. You will never get the victory in your own life behaving in such a manner.

> For where you have envy and selfish ambition, there you find disorder and every evil practice
>
> (James 3:16, NIV)

Time

Lack of quality time spent with God also results in spiritual heart disease. You are laying everything on the line by playing with this one. Do you expect to receive divine instructions from a God who you don't have time for? Ever met someone new and before you know it you are spending more and more time with him and less and less time with God? You may no longer pray the way that you used to. You may stop going to church like you used to. Your time spent with God eventually dwindles down to the point of nothing more than saying grace before meals in some instances. Is this intentional? More than likely no, it isn't. But if we're not careful, it's so easy to become sidetracked. Once you lose that connection with God, our sinful nature returns and it becomes very difficult to obtain balance. It becomes impossible to walk upright. The moment you stop feeding your spirit and begin to gratify your fleshly desires instead; you've missed it. Yes, you can date. Yes, you can fall in love. But how much are you willing to compromise in order to do so?

> For what shall it profit a man, if he shall gain the whole world, and lose his own soul?
>
> (Mark 8:36, KJV)

Luke Warm

> So, because you are lukewarm—neither hot nor cold—I am about to spit you out of my mouth.
>
> (Revelation 3:16, NIV)

A person who does not acknowledge God is "a dead man walking." He or she has no spiritual pulse. But what about those of us who *think* that we do have a relationship with God, you know, when it's convenient. This individual does spend time with God sometimes. He or she may throw up a prayer or two on a given day and definitely in times of despair. This person may attend church or may not. This person may even read a scripture or two at leisure. But, what type of spiritual life is this? There is no consistency. You're up one day and down the next. Hollering and crying and pleading with God one day to rescue you from "him" and then the next day because he apologizes and brings you breakfast you magically change your mind. You won't take the time required to really seek out God's will for your life so that you may gain the inner strength needed to do what is best. Instead you just "free style" your way through. In other words, "it's whatever." How can you expect to be in tune with God when there's an omission of fellowship? Do you think the Spirit of God is going to just hang around in a temple that is either unclean or that he is unwelcomed in? No, he will not. You can't just sit God on your front porch while your man is visiting. You kick God out in the cold...

turn on your favorite "grooves" and engage in "who knows what" with a man who nine times out of ten you don't have any business fooling with in the first place. This is no good. I trust and believe you will self-destruct over time. How do I know? Because I've been there and done all of that. And it took blood, sweat, tears, embarrassment, mockery, test, trials, and total deliverance to put me back together again. I was spiritually dead. I was looking good, talking good, but no good for anybody. Not even for myself. I had spiritual heart disease and was headed towards my end had I not called on the name of the Lord.

> No one can serve two masters; for either he will hate the one and love the other, or else he will be loyal to the one and despise the other. You cannot serve God and mammon.
>
> (Matthew 6:24, NKJV)

> For the wages of sin is death; but the gift of God is eternal life through Jesus Christ our Lord.
>
> (Romans 6:23, KJV)

Needless to say, we must learn to guard our hearts. Its role is far too vital for survival. We can no longer be careless as we once were.

> Keep thy heart with all diligence; for out of it are the issues of life.
>
> (Proverbs 4:23, KJV)

> That there were such a heart in them, that they would fear me, and keep all my commandments

> always, that it might be well with them and with their children forever.
>
> (Deut. 5:29, KJV)

Scripture says "keep your heart with all diligence." This means your heart must be protected at all times from possible external attacks. We must watch as well as pray. If we slip up, even for a moment, external issues (drama, foolishness, letting the wrong people in, etc.) can potentially contaminate the wellsprings of our hearts and subsequently affect our lives.

The Apostle Paul instructs us, "Finally, brothers and sisters, whatever is true, whatever is noble, whatever is right, whatever is pure, whatever is lovely, whatever is admirable—if anything is excellent or praiseworthy—think about such things" (Philippians 4:8, KJV). Dwelling on these things will help you keep your spiritual heart safe and secure. Your life depends on it.

The Heart vs. the Mind

Every Christian is locked in a constant, intense war with demonic forces. Sometimes we become so caught up with the external fight that we fail to realize that much of our battle is actually not external at all. Our most difficult battles often times are within our own minds and thoughts.

> But each person is tempted when they are dragged away by their own evil desire and enticed. Then, after desire has conceived, it gives birth to sin; and sin, when it is full-grown, gives birth to death. Don't be deceived, my dear brothers and sisters.
>
> (James 1:14–15, NKJV)

The Apostle Paul tells us to take every thought captive, so that it conforms to the will of God (2 Corinthians 10:3–5). So what's the mind have to do with the heart? Our minds have the ability to interpret and be made aware of how our heart really feels. The heart wants to do one thing and the mind wants to do another. Yet, the heart typically wins regardless of whether the decision is right or wrong. This state of constant internal strife causes us to do wrong even when we may want to do right unless we are guided by the Holy Spirit. A healthy heart makes healthy decisions. A diseased heart makes ill decisions. This is why you may want to end a particular relationship because in your normal reasoning you know it's no good for you, yet your heart keeps drawing you to the person. This is why your longing to be loved will lead you right into the hands of Mr. Wrong. Your heart desires something so badly that it will overpower your mental ability to make sound decisions. Your thought process becomes cloudy because of an overbearing urge within to get what you think will be good for you. Even if your potential mate does not meet any of your expectations, your longing to belong over time will supersede everything else.

The reason for this is better explained by the Apostle Paul in the book of Romans. Let's take a look at it in scripture:

> I do not understand what I do. For what I want to do I do not do, but what I hate I do. And if I do what I do not want to do, I agree that the law is good. As it is, it is no longer I myself who do it, but it is sin living in me. For I know that good itself does not dwell in me, that is, in my sinful nature... For I have the desire to do what is good, but I cannot carry it out. For I do not do the good I want to

> do, but the evil I do not want to do—this I keep on doing.
>
> (Romans 7:15–19, NIV)

As the Apostle Paul revealed, you will find yourself doing the wrong thing even when you have the best intentions.

Reflections

But someone will say, "You have faith, and I have works. Show me your faith without your works, and I will show you my faith by my works" (James 2:18, NKJV).

You believe that there is one God. You do well. Even the demons believe—and tremble! But do you want to know, O foolish man, that faith without works is dead? Was not Abraham our father justified by works when he offered Isaac his son on the altar? Do you see that faith was working together with his works, and by works faith was made perfect? And the Scripture was fulfilled which says, "Abraham believed God, and it was accounted to him for righteousness." And he was called the friend of God. You see then that a man is justified by works, and not by faith only. Faith without works is dead.

Do you have the faith needed to see yourself as the total package? Can you see yourself physically and spiritually healthy? Can you see the pep back in your step? Can you see yourself happy? Can you imagine yourself walking hand in hand with someone who truly loves God and then you? Isn't this the type of life that you desire? Well guess what? You can have it! All you have to do is believe God and ask for it. Begin to operate as if you already have yourself together with spirit led choices.

If anything in this chapter has brought conviction to you, let's thank God now. Perhaps as you were reading the thought may have crossed your mind "this applies to me." If so, there is no better time than now to invite the "master cardiologist" in to perform emergency surgery on you. He can put all of the broken pieces of your heart back together again. At this very moment you can be set free. It doesn't matter if you're in a crowded place or all alone. God sees you. He knows that you are wounded. He knows that you are broken. He knows that your heart is longing to be loved and respected. He knows what you need and exactly when you need it. Nothing is too hard for him. He's faithful. He is the one called able. Won't you open your heart to him? He can make you brand new at this very instant.

> He heals the brokenhearted and binds up their wounds.
>
> (Psalm 147:3, NIV)

Believe it or not, you can receive your deliverance right now in chapter one.

> Then will I sprinkle clean water upon you, and ye shall be clean; from all your filthiness, and from all your idols, will I cleanse you. A new heart also will I give you, and a new spirit will I put within you; and I will take away the stony heart out of your flesh, and I will give you an heart of flesh.
>
> (Ezekiel 36:25–26, KJV)

QUALITY CONTROL

> Quality is never an accident; it is always the result of high intention, sincere effort, intelligent direction and skillful execution; it represents the wise choice of many alternatives.
>
> —William A. Foster

My Story

We began dating around the second week of my ninth grade year. I was the new girl in my high school and was pretty much green to everything. I had no idea that I would be entangled with this man for the next sixteen years of my life. Thinking back to those early days, he never gave me the love and attention that I truly desired. At that time, I was not allowed to date anyway, so I passed it off as nothing. I can remember desperately trying to find ways to spend time with him outside of school. In my mind, this was love. To this day I cannot explain what made me fall so hard. From a teenager to a grown woman, my feelings only grew stronger. He turned out to be the bad-boy type, but I was hooked. It didn't matter. All I wanted was a life with him. My parents would've never approved of the relationship had they known from the beginning. And when my father did find out about him, he did everything that he could to keep me from him. Yet it only added fuel to the fire. I became pregnant at the age of seventeen. I can still remember the day that I found out. I was totally hysterical. I couldn't believe that this had happened to me. I had no idea of what to do. I rushed to his house to inform him of the news. He consoled me as I sobbed, and he assured me that everything would be okay. But you know what? He never again mentioned the fact that I was pregnant. He never asked how I was doing or if my parents were aware or anything. He acted as if I had said nothing. When I told my mother, she insisted that I abort the baby. I was totally against this, but at the time had no other choice. When I told him about my mother's plans, he never said a word. He never asked if a date had been set or anything. He erased the entire ordeal from his mind. Again, we were young, and I just assumed that he had his own way of dealing with things. Yet during this painful time, he began to walk another girl to class right in front of my face. But we were young, right? Well, this same behavior carried over into our adult life. He actually never changed. There were always other women. There was always a disconnect. He was never there when I needed him. He remained in constant trouble with the law. When I gave birth to our son three years later, he waited two days to come see him in the hospital. Then shortly after his birth, he spent a year in prison. During this time I cut him completely off and even married someone else. My husband at that time agreed to raise my son as his own and things actually went well for a while. Yet overtime I allowed the sweet lies of my former lover to confuse me. My marriage had a lot of issues, and I would like to think that neither of us was happy anyway. So after eight years of discontentment, I left my husband and went back to my first love. Keep in mind "my love" never had a job, was never able to provide, and was never there for me, yet I still went back. Within a matter of months he was back in jail again and I was left pregnant and alone again. While in prison, he again made me all of these false promises of wanting a family and wanting to do right by me and the children. He promised to never get in trouble again. He remained in prison this time for about ten months. Shortly after his release, the lies started again, the cheating started again, and again he never had time for the family. Since he never worked, I worked two jobs. One night when he failed to answer my repeated phone calls, I decided to leave work early and check on things. When I pulled up at home the garage was still up and the light was on as if he'd just made it in right before I did. I called his name as I walked inside but there no response. I then noticed a light on in my daughter's room near the back of the house. I thought to myself "that's odd. " I walked to the room and quickly saw the silhouette of a female running toward the closet. For a moment I felt like surely I didn't just see what I saw. Surely I didn't see a woman running to hide in my baby's closet. I went straight to the closet, and there she was. I can't find the words to describe the expression of horror on her face when her eyes met mine. As for him…he didn't even realize that I'd entered the room. He was too busy trying to find something entertaining for them to watch on the television. He quickly realized that he was "cold busted" or caught red-handed. You feel me? I had all of the evidence that I would ever need to be completely done with him. But guess what? I still didn't call it off. He begged and pleaded and claimed that it was all a big mistake. Of course I forgave him. I was in love, remember? Love conquers all, right? Wrong! All of this happened within two weeks of his release from jail. Within two months of his release, he again got in trouble with the law. But this time he was facing many years in prison. Even though I knew his track record, even though I knew that he had a pending court case, even though I caught him red-handed with another woman in my house where I paid all of the bills, I *still* married him. Yes. Yes. Yes…I married him. I honestly don't know what made me think that a piece of paper would change things. He didn't know God, so what did it mean to make vows with a God that he didn't even have a relationship with? Why did I think that he would change now because I was his wife? Things actually got worse. I was caught up in a whirlwind and had no idea of how to break free.

I would repeatedly ask myself, "How did I get here?" How could I be a career woman and a fool at the same time? How could I excel in one area of my life while plummeting in another area? This man displayed consistent behavior for more than fourteen years, yet I held on to a dream that somehow someday his actions and his words would align. Well, to fast-forward, his talk was cheap.

When it comes to the choices we make in our relationships, I often hear of women admitting that they settled for someone that they really didn't want or knew would not be the best fit. As I mentioned in my own testimony, he never gave me the love and attention that I truly desired. He never had a job. He was never there. He remained in constant trouble with the law. So why did I ignore all of the red flags? Why did I repeatedly make excuses for his consistent behavior? Could I not see that this man was no good for me? What makes us hang on when we know that more than likely the person we are involved with is not the best choice? Why do we wait until there are strings attached (feelings, children, etc.) before we really understand the magnitude of our mistake? Why do we build our relationships on a dream? Is it because secretly we like the challenge of trying to get a bad boy to love us? Think about it for a moment.

I knew early on that this guy was from a different walk of life than I was. He grew up unrestricted and could pretty much do whatever he wanted even as a ninth grader. I was raised totally opposite. Did I initially get a kick out of dating one of the most popular guys at school? Yes. Did I feel as if I had something that the other girls at school wanted? Yes, and honestly I enjoyed the challenge. There are many reasons why we "good girls" fall in love with "bad boys. " Let's discuss a few of them.

I Am Lovable

I grew up in an abusive home. My dad would snap out at any given moment. I've witnessed my mother being shot at, whipped with a belt while pregnant, choked, you name it. My sister and I have been chased with a pistol, dragged by our hair, punched, slapped, you name it. He was also verbally abusive on the regular. He would constantly remind me that I was going to be nothing just like my sister. He said it day in and out. He would often mock me at the dinner table. "Your lips are huge…you have a horse's mouth… watch how you chew!" Lord, I hated meal times. If we didn't make the beds just right, or wash the car just right, or mow the lawn just right…my sister and I were in for it. If he told us to do something and in his mind we didn't move fast enough or react as he expected, he would blow his top. It was as if he was never satisfied. Of course there was also this soft loving side that we got a chance to see after every one of his rampages. Yet, I never thought that I would live to become an adult. I knew for sure he would kill us all as he often promised to do. He even tortured us in the car. He would weave in and out of traffic going over one hundred miles per hour at all times. If my mother spoke up, he would drive faster and faster. My childhood was pure hell to make a long story short. I always promised myself that I would never become involved with someone who was abusive or had any of those tendencies like my father. Yet I did. So why is it so? When you are subject to abuse and that's all you know, you typically develop and inward sense of needing to "prove" that you really are lovable. This need carries over into your adult life, and you may subconsciously attempt to prove yourself by making a hard-to-get bad boy fall deeply in love with you.

I Finally Belong

Perhaps you grew up feeling as if you didn't belong. Were you the outcast of your family? Did you seem to be different than your other siblings? Were you treated differently than your other siblings? Do you look different than everyone else? Maybe you were adopted or not raised by your biological parents. Regardless of "the what" that caused you to develop a sense of rejection, it exists. When you carry that sense of not belonging over into your adult life, you may instantly become attracted to the first person who takes notice of you. You will be too blind to see that the guy is perhaps Mr. Wrong. You won't see that his intentions are impure. All you know is that for once someone has taken an interest in you. As a result you gravitate to that person. You overlook all of his issues. You simply want to be loved and in your own mind it seems as if someone has finally shown up and is willing to give you what you so desperately desire.

Man Improvement

There are some of us who fall for "bad boys" because we love the idea of "man improvement. " We typically fall for a guy with the intentions of making him "better. " For instance, we see the pants sagging yet we think in time he will love us enough to pull them up. We see the tattoos, the white tee, the gold grill or the missing teeth, the improper speech, and/or the disrespect he shows his mama, etc., yet we feel as if our love is powerful enough to alter his negative behaviors over time. We have this "love conquers all" mentality. Yet this typically does not happen. It can happen, but the odds are definitely stacked against us.

He Hates the World but Loves Me

Could it be that you actually enjoy the fact that your "bad boy" supposedly loves you but hates the rest of the world? Perhaps you are the only one who gets to see his softer intimate side. Yet it's only a matter of time before the behaviors that you witness him exhibiting to others are then exhibited to you. He is who he is. If he's snapping on the world, he will eventually snap on you. If he's irresponsible with money now, he will be irresponsible with money, even your money, later. If his credit is jacked up now, it will most likely be jacked up later. If he refuses to obey the law now, at some point he will likely find his new home inside of a prison cell or worse.

Let me harp on this for a moment; if your man does not have a job, then how can he take care of you? He can't bring anything to the table. Remember I worked two jobs to accommodate for his lack of not working at all? First of all, no real man is going to let his girlfriend or wife work two jobs while he sits around and does nothing. Hustling and bootlegging is not considered a job. Now if you're married and your husband gets laid off or something like that, then yes I can see you stepping up and handling things. After all, the two of you made vows. But for those of you who are in a situation similar to the one that I was in, survey says you should jump ship.

If there are children involved, things become even more complicated. Had I remained in that relationship for any longer than I did, my son would've thought that it was acceptable to go to jail, cheat on his wife, and allow his wife to work while he hangs out with friends. Children do know what's going on whether you believe it or not. This is why we have to be so careful when getting involved with someone. You don't want someone around your children who is not a good example, even if the parent is the biological father. It's sad but true. For years I felt terrible about my son not having a father. But you know what? I now realize that it was best. When the timing was truly right and my head finally got on straight, the Lord sent a God-fearing man into my household to help me train up the children in the way that they should go. He can do the same for you.

So what if you're already stuck? Well, I know this may be a hard pill to swallow, but sometimes we have to walk away from someone we have feelings for to get what we want in life.

Reflections

If this doesn't apply directly to you, I'm sure that it still hits close to home. It's far too common for you not to have a clue as to what I'm about to discuss.

1. How far can you expect your life to go if you're involved with a drug dealer? Everybody knows what time it is. Don't think that it's some kind of secret to all of those around you. Sure he may try to cover it up with a nine-to-five, but sometimes they become so bold that they don't even bother to do that. All the while you're enjoying all of the lavish gifts and name brand this and that but...it's only a matter of time before his luck runs out. At any moment your house could be subject to a drive by shooting. What if he owes someone money? How would you know? Don't think that his enemies aren't watching you. I don't care how nice he may be; I trust and believe somebody wants his blood. It could be a territory issue. Perhaps he's interrupting somebody else's cash flow. Whatever the scenario may be, you are playing a dangerous game. You are risking not only the quality of your life but life itself. If you have children, killers don't care. Children are left without parents all of the time. Or the killer may decide to torture and kill everybody including the innocent child. I hate to be so blunt, but it's time for us to get real. Is it really worth it? Is it worth your life? Is it worth

your sanity? Is it really worth it to become a prisoner in your own home? You never know when the U. S. Marshalls will come and beat down your door at 3 a. m. What about the random traffic stop with you in the car? They search the car...Surprise! There's a little package in the door frame that you knew nothing about. Who gets the charge? Both of you. The car gets impounded and your little one who's napping on the back seat is awakened to a social worker as she is transported to child protective services and then on to a foster home. And now you are locked up in the cell with "Big Bertha" who's talking about "you pretty. " Who's going to defend you? Who's going to save you? Where is your man now? And all for what? Is a Louis Vuitton bag really worth all of that? Do those Michael Kors shoes make you feel that good? Perhaps you're a Fendi girl. Is it worth it for the police to confiscate everything that you have and freeze all of your bank accounts? Even the ones that he thought no one knew about? Is it worth him going to jail for thirty years and leaving you behind to raise the kids? That's if you're one of the lucky ones. And how would you even begin to raise the kids considering the fact that you forfeited your dreams in order to ride on his magical red carpet. You don't even have a job, or if you do have a job it's not one that can sustain your lifestyle. So what's next? If you survive, he goes on to jail or to the grave, and you're left with nothing. Now those same folks that wanted to be in your circle cannot be found. You're all alone.

2. How far can you make it in life paying all of the bills because your man won't work? It isn't about the dollar per se, but it *is* about compatibility. He doesn't work remember? He has plenty of free time to surf the web and figure out ways to blow money. He pressures you to buy this and that. He's purchasing things day in and out while you're out making ends meet. He's a gambler or perhaps has a secret drug addiction. Before you know it, you have nothing. All because he doesn't know the value of money and has no concept of money management. What is in the top one or two reasons a couple divorces? Yes, financial issues. A couple that is never on the same page regarding finances from the very beginning has not much of a chance of surviving together for the long haul. If you're at odds now about anything serious, you will be at odds once you're married. For those who are married, I'm sure many can attest to the fact the many of the issues now were present before the marriage.

   Can two walk together, except they be agreed?

   (Amos 3:3, KJV)

3. How far do you expect an adulterous relationship to go? I'm sorry, but your man is borrowed. Borrowed means "you have to give him back" and "for limited time only. " He owes you nothing. You knew what it was when you subjected yourself to such foolishness in the first place. No good. No good. If both of you are married…guess what? You're destroying two households. You're both lying and scheming. You're both "double dipping" if you get what I'm saying.

And how do you convince your real man to take pills for an STD that you gave him. Or did he give it to you? Or did Mr. Loverman's wife give it to him who then gave it to you? Who knows? But wait, what if you contract something that a pill won't cure... now what? Not to mention you might get your skull cracked in this process or worse.

4. How far do you expect a homosexual relationship to go? This is not to step on anybody's toes. Yet, I would be remiss if I failed to mention this. I am not pointing fingers at anyone. I am simply speaking truth. Where's your fruit? Come on...think about it. This is not God's design. And what about your kids? How do you explain to them that your boyfriend is a girl? They are teased at school for this. You do know that right? And please don't get married to her. Isn't it a clue when you have to travel four states over to do so that this may not be the best thing for you? You're more than that. Stop limiting yourself based on a sexual preference, which resulted from a repressed heart condition.

So what's my point in all of this? God can deliver you out of any situation. But you have to acknowledge that what you are doing is wrong first. You may have been in a situation like this for a while, and it seems as if nothing bad has happened. But you know why nothing has happened yet? It's because sin can take decades to complete its work. Once sin is done, the result is death.

The bottom line is there has to be some type of quality control in order for a relationship to thrive. Even the folks who work in the produce section of a grocery store have to make certain that the fruits and vegetables that are put out are fresh. Most stores have timers set to release water to make certain that the foods are nurtured until purchased. Do you just go in there and pick up rotten apples and oranges? Do you not examine the product before you purchase it? So why are you just picking up any and everybody and trying to make them produce something that they can't. If he's rotten, he's just rotten. God has to deal with him. Not you.

Let me close out with this example of what can happen when we haphazardly get involved with someone or perhaps ignore the danger signs because we simply want to be loved. This is what can happen when there is a lack of quality control.

A Love Gone Wrong

A twenty-two-year-old woman was recently one of four victims involved in a quadruple homicide. She was shot execution style, along with her boyfriend and his cousin. A neighbor was also killed. I can still see the news clip in my mind portraying family members standing outside in the rain crying hysterically at the murder scene. There was yellow tape around two houses on a lonely dead end street that looked much like an alley. There were more police cars than I could count. I saw one of the velvet body bags being placed in the back of a sports utility vehicle for transport to a local funeral home. It seemed as if this was a scene from a horror movie. After seeing this, my heart became deeply troubled. I couldn't wrap my mind around the fact that someone had the audacity to walk into a home late at night and kill everyone in sight. There were no signs of forced entry. As the news repeatedly posted images of the victims, I couldn't help but notice the young woman. She stood out like a sore thumb. It was something about her smile. She looked so young and innocent. Yet this meant nothing to her killer. The gunman pointed the gun at the back of her head, pulled the trigger, and took her out just as he did the men. I would imagine that she begged for her life. I would imagine that she probably had nothing to do with whatever set the killer off. I would imagine that her boyfriend was right there next to her dead already or next in line. Such horror.

To make matters worse, a similar shooting occurred at the same house a few years ago. One of the men killed in this incident was wounded then. Another man was found dead in the front yard. The area was an obvious danger zone. So what was she doing there in the first place? Did she feel as if her boyfriend could protect her? I kept asking God why? I read the story over and over. I checked day and night for updates. I wanted answers. Why was there no mercy shown? How do we prevent this from happening to someone else? The only answer that kept ringing in my head was "warning comes before destruction." It is my prayer that what happened to this young lady serves as a wakeup call for the rest us. We always assume that we have more time to get things right. We for some reason feel as though we are exempt from the wiles of the enemy. Yet we are not. What happened to her could have happened to any of us if we place ourselves in that type of predicament. If he truly loves you, he will not place you in dangerous situations. Most importantly, if *you* truly love *yourself,* you will not place yourself in dangerous situations. If loving him places your life at risk, you must lay him aside. This young woman had her whole life ahead of her, yet it was snatched away in an instant. A single bullet ended her story.

> Therefore, since we are surrounded by such a huge crowd of witnesses to the life of faith, let us strip off every weight that slows us down, especially the sin that so easily trips us up. And let us run with endurance the race God has set before us.
>
> (Hebrews 12:1, NLT)

So where was my quality control? Why did I put up with so much? Had I been asked this a year or two ago my response would've been quite simple: "Because I was desperate and dumb." But you know what, God has since taken me on a journey and revealed to me what my true issues were. You see, I wasn't dumb after all, and neither are you. I was entangled in demonic bondage and could not free myself. If many of you could free yourself, you would be free already. We will talk more about this in the next chapter.

What I also had to realize is that I desired something that this man could never give me. We as women must realize that we cannot make someone be something that they are not. Regardless of what's being said, if his actions are not lining up with the words spoken, there will always be turmoil. You must want better for yourself.

> I am come that they might have life, and that they might have it more abundantly.
>
> (John 10:10, KJV)

SOUL TIES

Since we have these promises, beloved, let us cleanse ourselves from every defilement of body and spirit, bringing holiness to completion in the fear of God.

(2 Corinthians 7:1, ESV)

My Story

My mother was born and raised in Detroit. So each year, my sister and I were sent there for the summer to spend time with our grandparents and other family members. I can still remember the aroma of fresh pancakes on Saturday mornings when we visited my aunt's house. She would pretty much cook us whatever we wanted and would buy us whatever we wanted. I remember how each year she would mark our heights on the wall in the kitchen. From year to year we were able to see just how much we'd grown. I bet you that some of those markings are still on the wall today some thirty years later. Bitter-sweet memories.

I was about five years of age when it first happened. At this time, I knew nothing about homosexuality nor did I find it odd to have two aunts living in one house who also shared the same bed. I was upstairs watching cartoons in their bedroom when she (who I later realized was not a blood relative but a girlfriend to my biological aunt) came into the bedroom and lay down beside me. I trusted her. My parents and other family members did too. She began to hold me really close. Then she got back up and closed the bedroom door. She told me, "Okay, we're going to play a little game, but you can't tell anyone. " I remember saying, "Okay I won't tell. " And to this day—until now—I never told anyone. Why I didn't is beyond me. I can still remember her climbing on top of me as if it were yesterday. She then began to put her tongue inside of my mouth. She instructed me to do back to her what she was doing to me. So I did. Next she began to rub all over my body until she worked her way down below. She opened my legs and began to touch me down there. This went on for about twenty minutes or so. Of course I didn't understand what was happening. I didn't realize that a person that I trusted would take advantage of me. I had no idea of what sex was or what a lesbian was for that matter. I was clueless. Even the thought of it now makes me sick to my stomach. I kept this hidden for so long that's its actually still difficult to talk about.

Although she never touched me again, a deposit had already taken place. The following summer another female relative picked up where she left off, but this time I actually liked it. There was something in me that connected to something in her. We were both very young yet that spirit did not discriminate. I didn't understand what was driving me, and she probably didn't either. Those episodes went on for several years until we became older and realized something wasn't right. She actually stopped initiating things with me. And from that day to this one we never talked about it again, and it never happened again. Today, she is now a lesbian. Do you see a pattern here?

I didn't realize at that time what my so-called favorite aunt had actually done to me. It was more than just a physical act. It was far deeper than that. For almost thirty years, I never bothered to ask God why I had so many issues with men or why I felt weird when I came in contact with a lesbian spirit. It was as if something inside of me would leap when I met a woman who carried that same spirit. I fought this for years and years. If a saw a lesbian woman approaching me in a parking lot or say in a hallway at work, I would quickly drop my head. I did not want to make eye contact because I didn't want to feel anything as she passed by. Even as an adult from time to time I would give in to a lesbian experience. After the fact, I would feel so guilty and so dirty. It was as if I desired something that I really did not desire. I would fight it for a year or maybe even two, but then I would go back. I remember asking myself if I am gay. It became a struggle for me that I could not understand. Now by this point, I knew the Lord. I was in the church. Don't think that this type of thing only happens to people in the streets. There are plenty of "church folks" who are struggling with the spirit of homosexuality. For those of you who can secretly witness to what I am saying, it is a very difficult spirit to restrain from.

God gave me the revelation during midnight prayer one night after I asked him to reveal the root of the problem to me. I knew that I needed deliverance. He took me all the way back to the experience at the age of five. As the events began to replay in my mind, tears began to flow down my cheeks. I felt as if it were happening all over again. God explained that the moment my *aunt* began to kiss and touch me, a soul tie formed. She became my spiritual wife.

> So God abandoned them to do whatever shameful things their hearts desired. As a result, they did vile and degrading things with each other's bodies. They traded the truth about God for a lie. So they worshiped and served the things God created instead of the Creator himself, who is worthy of eternal praise! Amen. That is why God abandoned them to their shameful desires. Even the women turned against the natural way to have sex and instead indulged in sex with each other. And the men, instead of having normal sexual relations with women, burned with lust for each other. Men did shameful things with other men, and as a result of this sin, they suffered within themselves the penalty they deserved.
>
> (Romans 1:24–27, NLT)

Regardless of the excuses we as women make for developing dishonorable passions, there is a root to your actions and desires. You can choose to deal with it or keep pretending as if your lifestyle is okay. You can attempt to excuse your behaviors by attending a "gay church" or by proclaiming "God loves me. " Yes he does love you, and he's being very patient with you. But it's only a matter of time before his grace runs out. Eventually, you will receive the penalty deserved. I knew that what I felt and the actions to soothe those desires were displeasing to God. Yet, I had no idea of why this was happening or how to get out of it. You can blame the men who hurt you. You can blame whoever you want. Yet my advice would be for you to seek God concerning your situation. He knows exactly what you've gone through and how to bring you out. Somewhere down the line you developed a soul tie with a controlling, manipulative spirit. You have to discover it and break the tie.

What is a Soul Tie?

The Bible speaks of what is today known as soul ties. In the Bible, it doesn't use the term *soul tie*, but it speaks of them when it talks about souls being knit together. In its simplest form, a soul tie results when two souls tie together in the spirit realm. Not all soul ties are bad. For instance, soul ties between married couples actually draw the two closer together. The bond brings glory to God. Sexual relations between the two is an act of love and pleases the Father.

> For this cause shall a man leave his father and mother, and shall be joined unto his wife, and they two shall be one flesh.
>
> (Ephesians 5:31, KJV)

> What therefore God has joined together, let not man separate.
>
> (Mark 10: 9, ESV)

Those who engage in sex outside of marriage become one flesh, which God purposed solely for a husband and wife. The result is emotional bondage to a man or woman. A soul tie between two fornicators for instance can draw a wounded woman to a man who in the natural realm she would run from. But because of the demonic soul tie she runs to him instead. She realizes that he doesn't love her and treats her like a piece of trash, yet she can't seem to break free. She becomes magnetized to him. A soul tie with a lesbian spirit will draw you to a like spirit when in the natural realm you never would've imagined yourself in such a predicament.

> Do you not know that he who is joined to a harlot is one body with her? For 'The two', He says, 'shall become one flesh.
>
> (1 Cor 6:16, NKJV)

When a person has ungodly sexual relations (fornication, adultery, sodomy, rape, molestation) with another person, it can also result in soul fragmentation. The ties become destructive. Those who have engaged in such be it willingly or unwillingly will experience great difficulty bonding or joining with anyone in the future because their soul has become fragmented.

Susan's Story

This might be a new concept to you, but if you've been intimate in the past with someone other than your spouse and think back to that relationship even at the oddest of times, long for it, or dwell on it, that would be evidence that a soul tie exists. These ties can keep us from building true intimacy and trust with our spouses. It can also hold us hostage in an unhealthy place emotionally, spiritually, and sexually. When I was in high school, I found myself extremely promiscuous. I look back and realize that I was desperate for attention and seeking approval, which is something that I did not get at home. I began to engage in sexual relationships with different guys. I allowed them to use me for their own good pleasure. There were no limits. I even allowed myself to be used by multiple partners at the same time. I allowed them because in my mind I was finally getting the attention and approval that I so desperately needed. I created soul ties. And although those relationships were long over, I still found myself thinking back, remembering, and dwelling on the experiences. I would sometimes dream about the perverted things that they did to me and would want more. Sadly, these thoughts and visions continued even after I got married. I knew that I needed deliverance. I could not give myself completely to my husband because often times my mind would wander off someplace else. It was incredibly unhealthy. After seeking God concerning this, he revealed to me what was happening. I knew that these ties needed to be cut. If you have souls ties to the past and truly want to be free of them, ask God to cut and remove them. Let me warn you; this is nothing to be taken lightly. You need to mean business if you ask God to help you with this. Soul ties are very real and very serious things to God. Only God can cut what we have stupidly put in to place. To make a long story short, after my soul ties to the past were cut, I became trusting of my husband and built intimacy with him. I love him now more than ever and owe all of the glory to God. I am no longer reminded of the foolish acts of my past. I am free!

Godly soul ties can also result from close relationships such as the bond between King David and Jonathan. They had an authentic friendship.

> Now when he had finished speaking to Saul, the soul of Jonathan was knit to the soul of David, and Jonathan loved him as his own soul.
>
> (1 Samuel 18:1, NKJV)

Be mindful that soul ties can also form from bad relationships. This is why the company you keep is critical. If you link up with the wrong person you will soon find yourself picking up their bad habits and doing the ungodly things that they do. Although this is not your intention; a tie is formed and again a demonic force begins to drive you.

Signs that You May Have an Ungodly Soul Tie

1. You allow the person you are having sexual relations with to mistreat and abuse you. This can be physical or emotional abuse.
2. You can't get over the person even after the break up. The person is constantly on your mind.
3. You are still in a dead-end relationship and will practically do anything to keep it going.
4. The thought of the severed relationship brings you pain even after an extended period of time.
5. You cannot talk to or see the person without being drawn back to them even though the relationship has ended. So you go back, same result, go back, same result, and so on.

Breaking Soul Ties

I urge you to spend some time with the Lord so that you too may get to the root of your issues. There is a reason why you cling to the types of people that you cling to. There is a reason why certain people are attracted to you or why you are attracted to them. There is a reason why you may have found yourself in a relationship or marriage that you wouldn't have agreed to in a million years had not a demonic force manipulated you into that place. This is real. Ask God to reveal to you every ungodly soul tie ever formed. You must renounce every covenant that you've made knowingly or unknowing with the forces of darkness.

> For we wrestle not against flesh and blood, but against principalities, against powers, against the rulers of the darkness of this world, against spiritual wickedness in high place.
>
> (Ephesians 6:12, KJV)

Caution: Please do not do this unless you are serious. This is very important and not to be played around with. If you are not ready to break the ties or you need more time to reflect and identify with the information provided please come back to these instructions when you're ready.

1. Repent of any sins committed to cause the soul tie
2. Get rid of all connections with the person of which the soul tie was formed (wedding dress, keepsakes, rings, flowers, old letters, e-mails, text messages, pictures, etc.). Symbolization of what used to be can hold a soul tie in place.
3. Any vows or commitments made that played a part in forming the soul tie should be cancelled out,

repented of, and broken in Jesus's name. (I'll die without you, I'll never love another man the way that I love you, I am nothing without you, you are my life, etc.)

4. Forgive and move on. (This is the only way that you can get free from your own bondage).

BOUNDARIES

"No" is a complete sentence.

—Anne Lamott

Think about it this for a moment...

1. Is it acceptable for your man to not attend church, pray, or read the word and live a godly life?
2. Is it acceptable to date a man who is behind on child support?
3. Is it acceptable to date a man who drinks alcohol on the regular basis?
4. Is it acceptable to date a man who's married? Engaged? Openly involved with other woman?
5. Is it acceptable to remain involved with someone you've caught cheating?
6. Is it acceptable for your man to hang out with his boys excessively?
7. Should you have access to his cell phone/phonc records/e-mails?
8. Should you be allowed to answer his cell phone if you so choose?
9. Is it acceptable for your mate to curse at you?
10. Is it acceptable to be in an "open relationship"?

11. Is it acceptable for you to be in a same sex relationship? Involved with someone who is bisexual? For you to be bisexual?

Some of you may answer the above questions without a second thought. You may think that it's absurd to allow certain things to take place in your relationship. Others may not be so certain. Why? Because we as women often fail to set boundaries within a relationship. We are not upfront about what we will or won't tolerate, or we are unaware of our own preferences. When one is unclear about what is or what isn't permissible, it's only a matter of time before you're confronted with certain things that you may not feel so comfortable with. For instance, we may say that we will never date a married man yet somehow we find ourselves in a love triangle with someone else's husband. We may say that we will never cross the lines over into a same-sex relationship but next thing you know we've done the exact opposite. We may say that we would never become involved with a smoker, yet our potential prospect smokes three packs of cigarettes a day and a hookah pipe. So what am I saying here? In our self-driven quest for love we often times become uncertain. Remember the contentions between the heart and the mind that I mentioned back in chapter one? Well, here's a prime example. The heart wants to love while the mind wants to rationalize. You may sense that something is not quite right about the other person. You may know that you have no business getting involved with who you have chosen to get involved with. Yet, if you permit your desires to overpower your personal values, you will eventually settle for inappropriate behaviors and ungodly habits. You will put up with his foolishness knowing that you deserve far better. In my testimony in chapter two, I realized along the way that the guy that I was in love with was no good for me. Yet I continued to pursue the relationship. I wanted his heart so badly that I did all of the hoop jumping. I didn't count the cost. Nothing mattered. I behaved as if no other man on the face of the Earth could love me. I failed to set boundaries.

When no boundaries are set, the end result is a lost identity. Overtime it becomes all about what he wants. Everything is a *yes*. You will find yourself catering to him. If he tells you to jump, you ask how high. There is no challenge. You become completely predictable. All the while you think that you are doing all of these things to win him over for life. But in actuality, everything that you've done has simply confirmed to him that you have no mind of your own and have, therefore, been mentally eliminated as far as he's concerned. Without a sense of identity, the relationship goes nowhere. You lack the ability to communicate your needs and desires to your partner. So your partner rightfully assumes that you must not have any. Your partner then begins to determine who you are. This is when you get to that place of "I just can't imagine who I would be without him." You give up your sense of emotional security, you stop talking to friends, your integrity is lost, and there is no self-respect. You've become totally dependent on the other person for validation.

This is why it's best to set boundaries at the start of a relationship. You must tell the person what you will and will not accept in the event of an unkind or undesirable behavior. The tricky part is that you actually have to hold true to what you said you would do if something were to ever happen that violates those conditions. You must be mindful that you have total control over your own responses. Often times we say "If he ever hits me I'm gone" or "If he ever cheats I'm gone" yet when faced with the behavior; we don't hold up to our end of the deal. As a result, the other person develops a sense of security in knowing that they can pretty much repeat those same behaviors without having to face any consequences. If you're already involved or married it's not too late to come and reason together. It may be possible for your marriage to be salvaged or maybe not. I cannot speak on that but what I can suggest is for the two you to lay everything out on the table and establish what is and what isn't acceptable.

So, you jumped into a relationship without setting boundaries. Okay now what? Lets look at a real-life example of what can happen if we're not careful.

Michelle's Story

I met this African guy two years ago. At that time, he told me he had a wife. He said they weren't legally married, but she was the woman he intended to marry someday, so he felt comfortable referring to her as his wife. So at the time, I didn't mind. I felt like since she's all the way in Africa, it shouldn't have much effect on our relationship. It didn't take long before I fell in love with him. At the time, he was completing his residency. I knew shortly thereafter he would be financially secure. So in my mind, I was thinking, *Michelle just play your cards right and you too will be financially secure.* I often used my money to support him. I also gave him money to support his girlfriend in Africa. I did it because I loved him and wanted him to love me. I felt like I could handle him dealing with his girlfriend in Africa. Out of sight, out of mind right? But over time I became frustrated with the whole thing. If she called, he would talk to her as if I wasn't even in the room. He would go on and on about how much he loved her and how she is his queen. He would tell her things like "I can't wait for us to marry and start a family." All the while, I'm sitting there staring him in the face. He would go on and on for hours like this. All of his friends also referred to her as his wife. They often asked how things were going between the two of them and when would she be coming to the states right in front of me. I told him that all of this made me feel really low and I found it disrespectful. He responded by pointing to the door. He said if I had a problem with the relationship between him and his wife, I could leave. He reminded me that he was completely open and honest about her from the jump. He affirmed his intentions to marry her as soon as possible. He told me that she is the only woman that he has ever loved and will ever love. He told me that no one else could ever come between them. He reminded me that he did not love me and never will. Those words pierced my heart. I knew that I had to do something to win this man's love. Now I'll fast-forward a bit. About a year ago he planned a big trip to go visit her. During the two weeks he was away, he didn't call not even once to check on me. When he made it back, he told me that a wedding date had been set and would take place very soon. I panicked. I felt like my worst nightmare would soon come true. So I purposely slept with him and became pregnant. I stopped taking my birth control pills but did not tell him. I searched his phone one night and found her information. I then called her and gave her the news first. I told her that he was my man and that we were expecting a child. Of course she questioned him about it and then of course he questioned me about it. I told him that I was pregnant. He had no reaction. I expected him to be happy considering this would be his first born. He told me that he would accept his responsibilities but would never ever marry me. He told me that if I was the cause of his wife never talking to him again, he would never ever speak to me again. His sister found out about everything through his girlfriend. She then called me on the phone and told me that I disgust her. She said that I am nothing more than a "home wrecker." Next thing I know he buys his girlfriend a twenty-thousand-dollar ring and marries her. My heart was crushed. How could he choose her over me? I eventually gave birth to a son. I was alone in the delivery room and am alone now. He has made absolutely no contact with me since the marriage. He sends financial support for our child but that's about it. I don't understand how all of this happened. All I wanted was for him to love me.

As extreme as Michelle's story may sound, it's real. Yes we may say that we would never ever put ourselves in such a predicament, but you must be careful. When Satan has you all tricked up, there's no limit to what you will do. Remember, your reasoning is off under these circumstances. This guy told her from the beginning what his intentions were, yet she chose to accept it. Why? Because she had no boundaries. She was willing to do anything and everything for so-called love even if all the while he was in love with someone else. Time after time he made this clear to her, yet she held on to a hope that he would someday change his mind and marry her instead. She played the role of a fool and received a fool's reward. I hate to sound harsh, but it's true. Sometimes we become so desperate that we refute things that are actually true. His actions, words, thoughts, and deeds were consistent. He was in love with another woman. He simply dealt with Michelle for convenience. I don't know why in modern times women still believe that carrying a child for a man changes things. If you are married, of course the situation is different. But for those who are single, please don't try this. If he's going to stay then he's going to stay regardless. To make matters worse, we often try to "trap" him by doing such a thing. I mean come on now. I've had women admit to me that they became pregnant because they knew that the wife couldn't get pregnant. They purposely wanted to inflict pain. I've had others tell me that they faked pregnancies in a desperate attempt to gain his attention. But guess what, not one woman told me that this tactic worked. I mean, how low can you go? This is no different than any of us settling for being someone's mistress on the side. Do we think that we are of no more value than being a "fallback girl"? Do you like being somebody's plan B, C, or maybe even D? What makes you think that it's just you and her anyway? It's quite possible that he's running the same games all over town. What about when we find out that our man is involved with other women? Do you make the same mistake that I did and tell myself that since I'm number one it's okay. He'll eventually snap out of it. I remember his mother telling me: "*A man will be a man.* " Well, he can be a man all he wants, but he doesn't have to be my man. No! There is no way to find comfort in being number one of only God knows how many. Raise the bar. Set your standards and don't budge. In doing so, your man then has one of three options:

1. He realizes that his old, tired games won't work with you and quickly moves on.

2. He will respect your boundaries and never cross them.
3. He can pretend as if he respects your boundaries, cross them after he feels that enough time has passed, see what you do; and then if you forgive him and stay, he will allow more time to pass and cross those boundaries again.

It's just that simple. Our major problem is being afraid to express how we really feel. We think that if we come across too strongly, he'll leave. But guess what? If he leaves because you have self-respect, then good! He needed to go! Next! A real man desires a woman who respects herself. Trust me. He may play around with whomever but when it's time to make life changing decisions, he's no fool. He knows who he can bring home to his mama and who he can't. He knows who to tell his friends about and who to sweep under a rug. He knows who to take out to dinner parties and nights on the town. He also knows who to call at 11:30 p. m. because all of a sudden he wants to "see you. " Don't be that person! I've been there and done that. And what was my reward? A reality check as he walked back out of the door an hour or two later to his real woman. Then and there I am pleading with God to forgive me because I should know better.

In a healthy relationship, boundaries are strong enough, yet flexible enough, to allow us to be ourselves. Each partner brings respect to the table. No one becomes lost in the relationship. There is a sense of security.

The Word of God also confirms the need to set boundaries. I just love the Bible. Why? Because it contains a solution for any situation that you could ever face in life. Our father loves us so much that he left us a life guide. Every word is true. So while we're trying to do it our own way

God has clearly shown us his way. Then we wonder why we get the results that we get from doing it our own way. It can be compared to trying to put something together without reading the instructions. Ever done that? You put that new entertainment system together and then wonder why you have this bag still full of screws left over. It's because you missed some of the instructions and will not benefit entirely from your purchase. If you miss God's instructions, you will suffer. That's a promise.

Take it from me. Slow down and seek out God's will concerning a potential mate. If you're already married, God can make all things new. You have to decide what you want and then seek God concerning it. You must also be prepared to accept if somewhere along the way you missed it and made a poor decision. I finally had to walk away. Don't settle in an effort to please someone else. We have a heavenly father who sits high and looks low. He is who we should be aiming to please. The reward for seeking God wholeheartedly is beyond measure. Remember when we seek him first, everything else will be added.

EMPTY BED

> Learn your way around loneliness. Make a map of it. Sit with it, for once in your life. Welcome to the human experience. But never again use another person's body or emotions as a scratching post for your own unfulfilled yearnings.
>
> —Elizabeth Gilbert

Out of all of the reasons we often find ourselves trapped in a relationship, the fear of having an empty bed ranks at the top of the list. Personally, for many years and through many failed relationships, I just couldn't fathom the thought of being alone. I didn't want to turn over to a pillow every night. Even if he was coming home at 5 o'clock in the morning or not coming home some nights at all, at some point I knew he had to return home. I just couldn't let go due to the fear of being alone.

> For God hath not given us the spirit of fear; but of power, and of love, and of a sound mind.
>
> (2 Timothy 1:7, KJV)

I've heard that scripture many of times. I'm sure most of you have as well. Yet I didn't think it applied to my situation. I didn't bother to acknowledge the fact that I actually had a problem. It took years for me to finally admit that I was afraid of just being with Kellie. Was it because I didn't know who Kellie was? Was it because I allowed other people to define Kellie? Yes and Yes. So instead of telling the devil that he is a liar and that I can do better, I settled. I allowed him to convince me that I could not thrive on my own. I found myself in a downward spiral. It seemed as if every relationship that I became involved in pretty much ended the same way. I settled for behaviors that I was not comfortable with. I put up with individuals who were unfaithful. As much as I felt that I had to offer, some of those individuals would say, "I just don't want to be in a relationship…I don't want an emotional connection. " Yet, I even accepted that. Let me say this: it is better to be alone than to be with the wrong person.

As a result of my fear, I subconsciously made every effort that I could to make sure that I was never alone. When one relationship ended, I made sure that I had someone else lined up to fill that position. I had become a serial rebounder. What I failed to realize is that being alone does not equal loneliness. Being alone is not even a bad thing. Everyone needs time to find themselves. How can you expect someone to love you when you don't even know yourself? I thought I knew myself, but I had no clue. I didn't even know what I wanted. How can God give you the desires of your heart if you don't even know what it is that you truly desire?

I'm sure that many of you can relate to involvement in a "rebound" relationship. Sometimes it's someone you already know. There's this person that is patiently waiting in the background. He's aware of all of the chaos of your current relationship. He's supposedly "there for you. " There's no pressure. He swears that if he had the chance he wouldn't be foolish like the guy that you are with now. He may even help you escape your current relationship. He whispers all of the sweet nothings that you just feel the need to hear; regardless of whether you truly believe this wanna-be Prince Charming or not. You're already devastated with the idea of losing the so-called love of your life, so you fall for it.

If you move too quickly without being healed, you are going to find yourself "jumping out of the skillet and into the frying pan." There is no way around being alone. This is something that you must face in order to receive your restoration from the Lord. But remember, even when you feel as if you are alone you are not, God is always with you. He has promised in his word to never leave or forsake us (Hebrews 13:5). You cannot cushion the pain or bypass your grieving process by skipping from one person to the next. You have to take a time-out—*me* time—so you could learn from your experience, identify what failed, and be able to move forward. If you fail to do so, your new relationship will be short lived and could very well be worse than the last. A person who cannot be alone is at a significant risk of choosing anyone to avoid being alone. This is exactly what many of us have subconsciously done repeatedly.

We also carry baggage from the last relationship into the next one not realizing its impact. No one would want to purposely damage a new relationship with old issues. Yet until they are resolved, that is exactly what's going to happen. There must be time and distance between one relationship and the next. During this time, you must seek God like never before. He will reveal himself to you as well as his purposes and plans for your life.

I don't care how good the enemy may lead you to believe that this next person is. Please don't fall for this trick of deception even if this person is truly for you; until you go through your healing process, you will not be prepared spiritually or emotionally to take on something new. It will end in disaster. Trust me. Again, I am warning you *not* to rebound. I jumped out of one failed relationship to the next more times than I wish to count. It seemed as if I was getting away with my erratic behaviors until sin finally caught up with me. The errors of my ways allowed me to get myself into a situation that I will never forget—a situation that almost cost me everything including my life. Please understand I am in no way comfortable sharing all of my dark secrets with you. Yet I can't help you without dipping into my own business. I have to be real with you so that you can relate. I have to be open and honest with the hope that you will evaluate your own situation and make a decision to free yourself from captivity before its too late. This is nothing to play with. Life is too precious. The same as what happened to me or worse could happen to you. Please save your own life. Don't fall victim to this because of your fear of being alone.

My Story

After finally mustering up enough strength to end my second marriage, I again rebounded. I became involved with a guy who seemed to have himself pretty much together. He had his own home, his own vehicle, and a decent-paying job. He'd spent about ten years in jail (which should've been a red flag for me) but being the considerate person that I am, I figured he'd changed. Anybody can make a mistake, right? That's what I told myself. I'd also heard rumors of him abusing other women and having a terrible temper. But I guess I didn't believe it, or I felt as if he would never treat me in such a way. Besides, who believes rumors? One thing I can say is that there is at least a small portion of truth in the majority of lies that you hear. I should've dug a little deeper before falling face forward into the arms of an abuser. Hindsight is also twenty-twenty. Had I only known then what I know now. This is the very reason why I am writing to you. I pray that something in the text will tug on your heart and save you from destruction.

I knew that I would've never been strong enough to leave my current situation had I not had an outlet. So I assumed that this was my way out. I packed up my things, moved in with this other person, and immediately filed for divorce. At the time, I had small children, including an infant. I was already frustrated with the way things turned out with the man who'd made me so many false promises. Needless to say I was also vulnerable. Why do we think the grass is always greener on the other side? More often than not, this is pure illusion. Be mindful, never once did I consult God about this. Why? Because he would've told me no. Remember the word of God teaches us:

> Be anxious for nothing, but in everything by prayer and supplication, with thanksgiving, let your requests be made known to God; and the peace of God, which surpasses all understanding, will guard your hearts and minds through Christ Jesus.
>
> (Philippians 4:6–8, NKJV)

Is it just me or have you ever conveniently left God out of certain decisions and then convinced yourself that what you did was right? Now on with the story.

Things went well for a brief moment. We ended up moving quite a distance away from those we once knew. We had a new life together and had actually talked about getting married. Then the fighting began. The first time he hit me, I was actually driving us home from a party. He had been drinking, and I remember his speech being slurred. He was agitated and began screaming at me. I motioned to pull my truck over and as I did so, he reached over and punched me in my mouth twice. Out of fear I kept driving. I couldn't believe what had just happened. I wanted it all to be a dream. We'd just moved into a beautiful home and signed a twelve-month lease. I'd uprooted my children and left everything that I knew to be with him. So I felt stuck. I made excuses for him. I figured that since he was obviously drunk, it was an accident and would never happen again. I knew the classic symptoms of abuse. I knew the cycle. I knew all of the warning signs. I knew of the lies the abuser tells. Yet somehow, I became blinded to them or honestly thought something like this could never happen to me. The next morning he apologized and promised to never lay hands on me again. Foolishly I accepted his apology and attempted to put the entire ordeal behind me. Things got better for about a month or so. You know, the honeymoon phase. Then I began to notice more alarming behaviors. He began to display signs of paranoia and control. He would ramble through my cell phone and question me about every incoming and outgoing call. Yet I was not allowed to touch his phone under any circumstance. He even hacked my e-mail account. He began to question me about dirty clothes found in my gym bag, you name it. He would accuse me of flirting with other guys when we were out in public. Things had gotten so bad that I pretty much stopped going out with him. I preferred to stay around the house in an attempt to keep down confusion. I knew that I'd made a horrible mistake. I soon realized that I should've remained alone for a while. I was still hurting from the previous relationship while being emotionally and physically tormented in this one. I felt like I was about to lose my mind. I humbly thank God for his grace. It was he who kept me. Even in the midst of my sin, he shielded me. I didn't realize that the enemy of my soul had issued a death warrant on my life. I was just too blind to see it initially.

Needless to say, it happened again. He came home drunk again late one night and demanded sex. I refused. Of course this angered him. He then accused me of being involved with someone else and again started an argument. He became even angrier when I refused to engage in what he was talking about. I attempted to just ignore him and drift off to sleep, but he wouldn't drop it. He worked himself up and began hitting me again. I attempted to get away from him, but he pinned me down and would not let me get out of the bed. I couldn't believe that this was happening to me. He kept saying, "I want you to have my baby. " I was thinking in my mind, "Aint no way. " It's like a light bulb went off, and I remember thinking this man is really crazy, what in the world have I gotten myself into? I remember praying to God and asking for his help. I was praying that he would not rape me. And sure enough, he received a phone call and actually left me alone. I didn't care who the caller was. I was simply relieved. He left the room and slept on the couch. By morning he was sober and acted as if nothing had happened. By this time, I was heavily plotting my getaway. I didn't tell anyone in my family of the abuse. I kept to myself. I was ashamed.

Up until this point, none of the attacks had left visible bruises. Emotionally, yes I was scarred. But physically no one else could see. He continued to accuse me of being with someone else. He would pick fights with me anytime I went to church. He said that my church was a cult. I knew that I had to get away. We had about nine months left on our lease, so I didn't know what to do. He'd quit his job without even discussing it with me. He was no help around the house. I was living in a hell hole. It had become so bad that I was afraid to be alone with him.

I remember the last straw as if it were yesterday. About two weeks after the previous fight, he again stumbled into the house heavily intoxicated. His cousin was with him this time, so I figured I was safe, at least for the night. He stormed into the room awakening me from my sleep and accused me of being intimately involved with one of my good friends from high school. I was so confused. I didn't know where all of this was coming from. I tried to figure out what he was talking about, but he just got angrier and angrier. I remember him dragging me out of the bed, kicking me in my side and stomach. He dragged me from the bedroom to the living room by my hair. I was screaming for his cousin to help, but the cousin was too afraid. He began punching me in my head and everything went black. I saw stars, and I can remember thinking he was going to kill me. To make matters worse, he did say he was going to kill me. I remember attempting to fight back, but it was no use. He was much larger than me. He dragged me all over the house. Kicking, punching, and beating me, all while promising to kill me. Somehow I eventually slipped out of his grasp and began running toward the garage. I began banging on the door to the room where the cousin was. I begged for him to let me in. Finally, he did. I locked the door behind me. That meant nothing, my abuser simply kicked down the door. I felt like I was in a movie or something. You hear about these things on TV. You see sad stories on the news. But never in a million years would I have pictured myself going out like this. I was a career woman. I attended church. Yet, there I was fighting for my life. With the cousin attempting to calm him down, I remember him giving me one last kick. Then he stood over me a moment while his mouth collected enough saliva. He hocked back and spit right in my face. He told me that I was nothing but used much stronger words. He treated me as if I were a stray dog, if not worse. So there I was, with my face black and blue. That was it for me. A day or two later, I broke my lease and moved into an apartment back in my home town. He continued to stalk and harass me. But I was done. By this time, I was with Jesus all the way, and I knew that I had been forgiven. I knew that God was with me and I did not let fear stop me from doing what was needed. I obtained a peace bond on him. That meant nothing. Finally, after about ten emergency (911) calls because of his stalking and threats, he left me alone. You know that when you listen to the voice of God, he will protect you? You don't have to be afraid. When the enemy comes one way, he will have to flee seven ways (Deut 28:7). God being for you is greater than the entire world against you (Romans 8:31). God kept that promise to me and will do the same for you. It took months for the blood vessels in and around my eyes to heal. But it took years for my heart to heal.

I learned a very painful lesson through all of this. Don't move without God. Don't jump into another situation because of your fears of confronting your own issues. Had the Lord not intervened, I would not be alive to tell my story today. My children would be motherless. It's a lot to think about. Please consult the Lord before you make any life-changing decision. If he tells you no, it's for good reason.

FRUITS OF MY LABOR

> Give but don't allow yourself to be used. Love but don't allow your heart to be abused. Trust but don't be naïve. Listen to others but don't lose your own voice.
>
> —author unknown

Lisa's Story

I met my first true love on the first day of my freshman year of college. I wasn't looking for love at the time and was actually caught off guard. Jarrod and I started off as best friends. He was silly and spontaneous. There was never a dull moment. I was his first girlfriend, and he was my first serious boyfriend. Yes, I'd dated a few guys in high school, but it was never anything official. As our relationship grew, we became inseparable. We met each other's families, went on trips together, and spent little to no time apart. I felt as if I could not breathe without him and often freely expressed that to him. We balanced each other.

Everything was perfect for about two years. Yes we had our ups and downs but overall we were good. We'd even talked about getting married and starting a family after graduation. I would talk about moving to a big city like

Chicago where there would be work opportunities for us both. He never once gave me the indication that he and I were not on the same page. Then all of sudden things changed. I went away to visit my family for the holidays and upon return he seemed distant. He came to my apartment one night and just flat out told me he was in love with someone else. He told me that he needed space and some time to think. I began crying hysterically and asking what I did to turn him away. He could only say that he loved me but didn't want me. I was crushed. My entire world came tumbling down all at once.

I began seeing a therapist but all the while I kept trying to figure out a way to get the love of my life back. I did everything for him. I was always supportive of his dreams and visions. I quickly corrected anything that he didn't approve of. I gave up my friends. I spent less time with my family. I just couldn't make sense of it. Why did he not want to be with me? As time went on, I would repeatedly ask him what needed to be done in order to get things back to the way they used to be. He finally told me that during our relationship, I was too needy and took up way too much of his time. He said I pressured him and repeatedly talked about the future. He said he felt much more relaxed with his new girlfriend. He told me that he no longer loved me and that his heart belonged to someone else. After that conversation he stopped answering my calls altogether. If I saw him out on campus he acted as if he never knew me. Yet I still could not let go.

I thought about how I'd bent over backwards to make him happy for the past two years. I gave up my own opinion about so many things in an effort to maintain his love. I'd become lost in him, and he knew it. It now feels as though our two-year relationship meant nothing to him. I don't think he ever truly appreciated the extent to which I went to love him. I don't think he ever fully understood how special our relationship was. I loved him with all my heart and soul. I forsook everything for him. I gave him my very best yet even that wasn't good enough. My love wasn't strong enough, and he found someone else and moved on so quickly. I just keep hoping that he'll realize this was all a big mistake and come back to me. How could I put in so much and get nothing but a broken heart in return? I know that I should move on yet I'm stuck. My life is on hold. I'm so afraid that he thinks his life is much better without me. I made him who he is. I groomed him. How could another woman just waltz in and reap the fruit of my labor?

Can you relate to Lisa's story? I sure can. Ever been in a relationship where you give your all and he turns around and moves on to the next woman with little to no explanation given to you. I was once involved with someone who strung me along only to look me in my face months later and tell me that he was about to marry someone else. So there I was sitting on his couch with my mouth hanging open, wondering where in the world had this other woman been for the last year almost. I remember feeling "plucked. " I was so shamed! My face was red, and my eyes instantly filled with tears. I had done everything to gain this man's attention. I would've jumped over the moon if he'd asked. I prepared meals for him. I ran errands for him. I even took cooking lessons in an effort to please him because our cultures were different. If he had a headache or sinus infection, I would hurry to bring him medication. I did his grocery shopping. I did everything within my power to let this man know how much he meant to me. I loved his conversation. Sometimes we would talk for hours. If he had an important engagement, he acted as if he could not go without me. I met his family, his friends, his pastor, and so forth yet in the end he told me he was soon to marry another woman. I remember the words echoing in my head "I'm about to get married." I jumped up from his sofa and stormed out. I remember slamming the door. I got into my car and said, "God, I know that you're going to do something with this situation." I knew that God was not going to let me go out like that. At this point, I thought that I'd put all of the silly stuff behind me. I was living a consecrated life. I spent hours and hours in prayer a night. I had broken every soul tie. Every male from my past had been cut off. I disappeared from social media. I was fasting at least twice a month. I was doing everything within my power to prevent history from repeating itself. I thought, surely this man had to be the one. He was saved, intelligent, and wealthy. We talked about the goodness of the Lord together. He knew the scriptures fluently. He wanted me to attend his church weekly. Yet, he forgot to mention one important thing to me—his engagement. Looking back, I now realize that it was all in my head. A day after his announcement, he phoned me and asked why I responded the way that I did. Why was I not happy for him? I told him that I was deeply hurt. His response is something that I will never forget. It is also the point of this entire chapter. He boldly told me, "You hurt yourself." And you know what, he was right. I bent over backwards but never once did he reciprocate anything that I'd done. I placed myself in a vulnerable position. He never once told me that he was going to spend the rest of his life with me. I spent months hoping for something that would never ever come to pass. I spent months catering to his every need when all along he had no intentions of being with me. Yes I ended up hurt, but it was a result of my wrong investment. Lesson learned.

As women, we are typically more invested in our relationships than men. Our happiness is predicated upon how well things are going in the relationship. If he's not happy, we're not happy. In order to keep him happy, we will do just about anything. Think about it. Who typically recognizes when things in a relationship are not going so well? We do. Who typically suggests counseling when it seems as if professional intervention must take place? We do. Who is willing to travel near and far to attend relationship seminars or church conferences in order to save our relationships? Yes, women. Given, women are biologically wired to be the nurturer of the relationship. This is the way that the Almighty God designed us. We have been programmed to anticipate the needs of our mate. Yet, where do we draw the line? Is there not a cutoff point? Often times, even before marriage, we give our boyfriends husband privileges. We cook, clean, build their credit, open joint accounts, buy lavish gifts, change ourselves, all to make someone happy who may not even be our husband in the first place. Even if the person that you are involved with appears to be husband material, that doesn't equate to him being the husband for you. Not only that, but majority of the time we invest everything that we've got into someone who we have absolutely no business marrying in the first place. That or he has no intent whatsoever of marrying you. Why do we give so much of ourselves? Is it because we are desperately trying to prove to him that we are wifely material? When you give your all to a man who is not even your husband, how much of you do you have left for yourself? Then when he abruptly walks away, there you are left in a state of depression. He picks up his life in about two seconds flat, goes on, and marries the next woman. But there you are, still wondering what went wrong and why couldn't he see what a great woman you are. Six months later your head is still in the clouds, believing that he's just going through something and will soon come back to you. You basically place your life on hold as his life fast forwards.

Relationships are give and take. It should not be you giving 100 percent while he gives zero. It's something that you two have to achieve together. If he's not giving you 50 percent now, how much do you think he will give you if he was to become your husband? There must be a common goal of sticking together no matter what. Each should have the other person's best interest at heart. If the foundation of your relationship is not healthy, you will not generate positive equity. Over time, a deficit will take place. You will end up walking away with less than what you started with.

I'm not speaking of finances in this regard. I am speaking of an emotional return on your investment (ROI). You will lose out. You will be robbed of your self-esteem, your trust, your hopes, and dreams. Not to mention the amount of energy you will spend attempting to make the relationship work. If your self-esteem is destroyed, it can take years to re-build, if it rebuilds at all.

So what do you do when the so-called love of your life moves on? Do you just press the pause button on your own life? I pray that your answer is no. Do you just sit and wait because you're the one who trained him to be a good partner in the first place? No, you don't. Sure you fixed him up. Sure you made him better. Sure another woman is now reaping the fruit of your labor. Well, so what? Move on! The ugly truth is this—you were not the one. Even if at one time he told you that you were or led you to believe that you were. This is something that you must accept in order to go on and get God's best for your life.

I often hear woman stating, "The timing just wasn't right. " Maybe if we'd met a little later, things would have turned out differently. Well I don't agree with that. I think that timing has very little to do with it. If it did, he wouldn't have so readily jumped into something else. It's difficult to accept that someone does not want to be with you. It causes pain and distress. Yet, the quicker you can accept it, the sooner your healing process can begin. There's no point in being upset over someone just because we can no longer have them. Yes it will hurt, but deal with it and move on. Besides, far better is being prepared for you. You have to believe it even though you can't see it right now.

But as it is written:

> Eye has not seen, nor ear heard, Nor have entered into the heart of man. The things which God has prepared for those who love Him.
>
> (1 Corinthians 2:9, NKJV)

CHAMELEON

> I don't know why he gets to be two people, and I only get to be me, the one who is here to take what he has to give, and who is here to pick up the pieces afterward.
>
> —Amanda Grace

Summer's Story

It's been difficult to focus on the things that I should because I've been reflecting on all of the pain. No matter how much I think about it, it does not ease or diminish in any way. It seems to deepen and widen like an abyss that grows daily. How do I get out? I loved this man with all that I am and could ever hope to be. He appeared to be the answer to my prayers. He was funny, kind, sweet, intelligent, expressive, emotionally available, and reflective. He used to love that I asked deeper questions; he said that it made his mind tingle and that he realized he was dealing with a real woman and not a little girl. The courtship was new and sweet, watching movies, cuddling, and sweet kisses, with the resolve to refrain from having premarital sex. I appreciated that. As we got closer, I showed him my true self and let him know what my boundaries were as he had several female friends. As we were developing into a relationship, I felt it was important to be upfront about these things that could potentially become problems. There was a girl who he had been physical with but denied having intercourse with who was ever present in his life. Something of which, I could not tolerate. It took a long six grueling months before I saw physical proof that he had finally told her to stop contacting him. Then still, he did not offer an explanation to her or be clear with her concerning his so-called desires to protect me or our new relationship. Of course, this left me feeling vulnerable and insecure. If I meant so much, why would you gamble with your potential life partner over a friend who claimed to be in a committed relationship with someone else? I always wondered how strong his feelings were for her because I felt he must love her to fight to keep her around even at my expense. There were other things before this. There was a female who he had had intercourse with whose number appeared in a new phone, but contact between them supposedly ended two to three months before. There was another woman who solicited him for sex before I met him, yet he never contacted her to say the thing is off he's in a committed relationship. Then there's the friend who casually shows up to go with him to the grocery store when he wanted to bake me a surprise...why was she there? It seems that a man who verbalizes his desires and boundaries within the relationship would act accordingly... that is, treat me the way he wants to be treated. Come to think about it, his level of follow through has never been great, the follow up either. I'm still waiting on him to pay half on the cable bill from when I was staying at his home temporarily. Now that I have my own home, I am still waiting on half on the furniture that was purchased months ago. It all boils down to. . . . I am still waiting for a change. . .

Those are not the big things that plague my mind throughout the course of the day. Morally we both knew and discussed the importance of heading our relationship in the right way, but we eventually gave way to our flesh and engaged in premarital sex. Things actually worsened after that. He was more distant, less affectionate, so I suspected another woman. My suspicions were later confirmed. Well actually it was worse than I could've imagined them to be. He stooped so low. I mean the thought of it now still disgusts me. One evening I checked his e-mail on a phone that was supposedly used for the sole purpose of listening to music only to find a generated e-mail that contained this message:

> Hi sugar, I am available today, tonight, and through the weekend. I offer many services and am willing to customize your own special package. Hope you're ready for more good news. You can go as many times as you wish during our date! I have a nice cozy hotel suite right now but I can also come to you if you wish! I am having a $150 in-call special this week and a $175 out call special for 1 hour. For 30 mins its $100 in-call and $125 out- call. . . . If you have any fetishes or requests we can discuss them before our date. . .

Mind you my mouth gapped open, and I began to hyperventilate before bursting into tears. This e-mail was dated a few months before we had met but just the thought that this man, my man who I held in such high esteem, who I just decided to lay with was capable of soliciting a prostitute sickened me to my core. It's bad enough to pick up some chic from the streets or fool around with a so-called friend from the past. But to actually, purposefully, knowingly get with a prostitute is in my opinion was the epitome of perversion. This e-mail came in less than four months prior to us being official. I did not actually find the new one, ...another one, just like the one above until a month after it was sent; that is, three months into our relationship. So, by this point I've compromised my morals, catered to this man, stayed through inappropriate contact with his past sexual partners, and dealt with his jealousy of people due to his perception of my crossed boundaries, and this is how he repays me. But do I leave him? Nope. You would think that by the third time I found proof of him again soliciting a prostitution service I would've had enough. This time we were fourteen months into the relationship. Moral of the story: what is wrong with me to put up with a lying, conniving, selfish, morally-inept man who does not know what God's love is or what respect is? I ask for anyone who reads this to keep praying for my deliverance for it is coming. The warning signs were there from the beginning, but I chose to ignore them. He did just enough sweet thoughtful things to reel me in and show me what he wanted me to see. I asked myself several times, and I asked him if this relationship is what he really wanted and if he was ready for what I am ready for. Each time he said yes. Alas, I'm here pregnant by a man I don't like and don't trust, but he insists that he loves me and wants to marry me. Of course, he repeatedly denies ever actually sleeping with any of them. So why would he contact them on at least three separate occasions? This man is a chameleon. He's one way in front of my face and then a totally different person when my back is turned. Or are lies and acts of perversion the real him and here I am just too blind to see. Perhaps he's not a chameleon at all. Perhaps I am only seeing what I want to see. I honestly don't know who I fell in love with. Even talking about it causes my eyes to sting as they fill with tears. I'm telling my story in hopes that another sister can relate and also break free.

Does the person that you are so in love with truly change or over time does the real person simply emerge? I believe that it's the latter of the two. You can only pretend to be a certain way for so long. Over time, the temporary you will revert back to the real you. When the individual does all of the things needed to reel you in, they have simply and momentarily stepped outside of their real character. The person that you are actually drawn to is *not* who they really are. As difficult as this is to accept, this concept has been proven true time and again. We find ourselves hanging on to what once was in hopes of seeing those same loving, trusting behaviors again. Ever noticed that even when they have so-called agreed to change back into the person that they used to be, it typically only last for about a week or two, or maybe even a month. Again it's simply a short-term transition, which is why before you know it they are back to doing the same old things again.

It is totally exhausting to try to change someone or to sit around in wait for your man to magically transform into your knight in shining armor. It's exhausting because it is not possible. The only person that we can change is ourselves. Please stop thinking that you are the one that can change him against all odds. Yes it's a challenge, but in the end you will lose. Let him go be with someone who can accept his games. There is not a man shortage in spite of what you may hear. You don't have to break your neck or jump over a fence to get your man to care enough about the relationship to change. If he cares, he will do what it takes to sustain the relationship from start to finish. He will not do things that he knows darn well he would not accept from you. So if he will not accept the lies and schemes from you, don't accept them from him. A person who respects a commitment will do just that. You don't have to mope around crying crocodile tears because he's still flirting with an ex. A man who truly cares about you will not fathom the thought of doing those things to you in the first place. A man who truly loves you will not disrespect you. If it happens unintentionally, he will quickly correct the problem.

True enough you may be the catalyst for someone's change. You know how later on you may hear that the man you thought for sure would be yours forever is now happily married to someone else. Well, the key word here is *catalyst*, not *you're it*. Even players fall in love and settle down eventually, but he typically does not settle down with the woman who put up with all of his idiocy. Your walking away may force him to wake up and smell the coffee. It may inspire him to find truth within himself. But I advise you to keep walking. Don't walk away with the hopes that he will instantly change, want you back, and then you all live happily ever after. No, Ma'am. You're not Alice, and this is not Wonderland.

Please be honest with yourself. If you are in a relationship where you are desperately hoping to change him in one way or other, these are your options.

1. Accept him the way that he is and find peace. That means no more arguing about his changing or cry-

ing because he is not demonstrating the actions that you've requested a million times already.

2. Love him enough to let go. Accept that you don't have a magic wand that you can wave over him and see change. Walk away peacefully. Don't key up his car on your way out of the door.

Remember, accepting that your partner will not change is the first step. No more dreaming and hoping. It is what it is. It does not mean that you have failed in anyway. It means that you have matured to a place that most people truly struggle with. I've talked to so many women who've expressed regret for not facing the truth sooner and calling it quits. I wasted half of my life hanging on to a hope that never came to pass. You have the power to change the way your story ends. It may seem as if you are losing but in all actuality you are winning. You are deserving of a man who shares your values. You are enough exactly as you are. You don't have to jump through hoops—no more begging and pleading. No more ultimatums. If he is not changing or making considerable strides in the way that you are requesting, that is not your fault. Love cannot heal everything. It is not your responsibility to fix anyone else's issues; every man for himself. Respect him enough to allow him to find himself in his own timing. Please reverse your energy. Put your all into loving and developing you. The change that we desire from our mate is often times a mirror image of what we actually need for our own transformation.

Casey's Story

I have to believe that I am going through this so that someday God will use me to help someone else. I look back over my life and realize that I should already be sleeping in my grave. But God loved me in spite of everything. He gave me the strength to finally accept things for the way that they truly are. I never thought that my life would become one of those stories that you read about. I always figured that certain things simply could not happen to me. I certainly did not think that I could become a victim in my own home.

I finally gathered up the courage to leave my emotionally, physically, and sexually abusive husband of three years. We'd been together for ten. It breaks my heart that I brought my kids into this situation—they are fifteen-month-old twins. I realized that I had to get out for my safety and theirs.

My husband started to emotionally abuse me after about three months of dating. I was young and in love and believed he could change. Ten years, countless breakups and reconciliations, countless trips to the emergency room, countless rapes, and two children later, something inside of me finally clicked. I finally listened to the Holy Spirit, who I now realize had been speaking all along. I finally became strengthened enough to leave this person who has made me miserable for the past decade. I've been so miserable to the point I couldn't even bring myself to eat. I've had multiple suicide attempts, but each time God intervened. I wasn't sure how my story would end. I didn't know if he would kill me, or I would kill myself first. I began to hate myself. I blamed myself for his actions. I felt like if I could just be a better wife he would change back to the person he was when we first met. Yet those dreams have long ago been replaced with nightmares—nightmares that became my reality. I realized that this man would never change and if I didn't accept it I was going to soon lose my life. I remember feeling so mixed up in the head. He would twist things to such a degree that I could no longer think straight. Every time I would look at him, all I could see was a red, angry face. His eyes filled with rage. He would force me to do all kinds of perverted sexual acts while repeatedly saying "You are a harlot, nothing but a thankless whore" or "You are a failure. You should've been aborted" or " You are worthless." Then the next day he would turn around and try to convince me that he is trying to change. Not long ago he ripped out a chunk of my hair right in front of one of his friends. Then he sent me to our room where he continued to physically abuse me. The result of that beating was a punctured lung.

I am writing this as a warning to others. Not everyone is able to live to tell their story. If you are in a situation where you've seen the warning signs but have ignored them in hopes that he will change. Please get out now. Don't play Russian roulette with your life.

I pray that Summer's and Casey's stories will help you to realize how damaging it can be to wait on someone to change only to finally realize that they never will. At least not during the lifetime of your relationship. They both saw the warning signs but chose to ignore them in hopes that transformation would come. Many of us have been in this position or are in it right now. You have to realize that change can be a force for power and progress; but if mishandled, it can be a force for stagnation and regression. Please do not allow anyone else to hold you back. Your growth becomes stunted when you devote all of your efforts into trying to change someone else. I foolishly prayed to God to change him for many years and through many relationships. What was my end result? No change. We must remember that God is the bedrock of our peace; the source of our strength. His desire is for us to live a life that is progressive and fulfilled. Every good and perfect gift comes from him (James 1:17). If you're losing your mind while waiting on someone's change, God most likely didn't send him in the first place. Accept that you are not mighty woman. God will bless you with your heart's desire if you trust him. Please let go and let God.

THE DECEIVER

Just because something isn't a lie does not mean that it isn't deceptive. A liar knows that he is a liar, but one who speaks mere portions of truth in order to deceive is a craftsman of destruction.

—Criss Jami

Karman's Story

I was on business travel with my corporate job when I first met David. We actually met in the airport. For me, it was love at first sight. David was quite a looker: tall, well dressed, and he smelled so good. His skin was perfect and so was his hair. His smile was worth a million bucks. We had instant chemistry and impeccable conversation. I just felt like he was the one. He too was high up on the corporate ladder. He had a six-figure income to match mine. Everything seemed to just fall right in place. We dated for about a year and then married. My wedding was better than any fairy tale that I'd ever seen. For our honeymoon, we spent a month in Paris. I felt like the luckiest woman alive.

Things went seemingly perfect for the first six months. I couldn't have asked for more attention or more of anything for that matter. Then all of a sudden my world flipped upside down. I was getting ready for the gym one morning and noticed that my husband wasn't looking so well. He complained of feeling "weak." I checked his temperature to find that it was a dangerous 104 degrees. He said it felt as if he had the flu or something. I gave him something for the fever and insisted that he be seen by a doctor, but David refused. He said it was nothing and would pass. He finally agreed that he would go in if he was not better in a few days. Over the next week or so, David began to feel better. So I agreed that it must've been nothing. About two weeks later, I ironically began to experience the same flu-like symptoms. I felt it was a bit odd so I immediately scheduled an appointment with my family doctor. I explained the symptoms and told him that I wanted to be checked for "everything." He asked me if that included HIV, and I said, "Yes, everything." I left the doctor's office and was told that I would get the results in about a week. Just as David, my symptoms went away within a few days, and it seemed as if things were returning to normal. But that's when I received the phone call that no one would ever want to get. The doctor's office called and asked me to come in for my test results. My heart sank. It was then that I was told that I indeed tested positive for HIV. I didn't know what to think or how to begin to wrap my mind around such. How would I explain this to my husband? Did I give this to him? I remember feeling so guilty. When I made it home, I hysterically told him the news. I remember him rubbing my back and telling me that it's okay. I couldn't believe how calmly he reacted to such horrifying news. David agreed to go in for testing and a week later was also informed of his HIV positive status. The next two years of our marriage was very difficult. We rarely talked and were no longer intimate.

I had been hiding our secret from everyone. I'd become totally disengaged from family and friends. I was so tired of the way that I was living but of course I couldn't walk away. The thought of me giving this to my husband was just something that I could not get past.

One evening I came home from work a few minutes early and noticed that David's laptop was open on the couch. I really didn't think much of it. I plopped down next to it and began drifting off to sleep. I was tired both mentally and physically. I heard an alert sound on his computer indicating that he had a new e-mail message. I glanced at the message flash and noticed in the subject column it said, "Married HIV positive man seeking sex from HIV positive man." My heart dropped. I hurried upstairs and found David in the study. He appeared startled at my coming home earlier than expected. I calmly asked him a question that no woman would ever want to ask her husband.

"David, how many men have you slept with?"

David paused for a moment and then said, "Six."

My entire body went numb. He confirmed that his last intimate encounter with a man was a couple of weeks before he came down with those flu-like symptoms. So in actuality, David passed HIV on to me. To anyone who is reading this...please know that this can happen to you. HIV/AIDS does not discriminate. It doesn't matter how smart you are or how rich you are. It doesn't matter how good looking he may be or how good he may smell. You had better know what you are getting involved with. Never once did I consult God before jumping into the relationship. It just felt so right. Remember the heart is deceitful. Just because something may initially feel right does not mean that it is. Satan knows what we like and how to reel us in so perfectly. My "Prince Charming" issued me a death sentence. He deceived me. Please don't let this happen to you. Count the cost.

A deceitful man will do whatever it takes to get what he wants. He doesn't care who he hurts. He doesn't care what he has to tell you. He knows how to walk the walk and talk the talk. He knows how to play his cards right until he gets you right where he wants you. So where do we as women often go wrong? First, many of us never ask the appropriate questions from the start. Karman admits to never asking David's HIV status prior to the marriage. Everything "seemed" so right that she dared not insult him with such a question. Do we actually ask our potentials of their HIV status? Do we even know our own status? Do we ask of their criminal history? Do we ask if they've ever hit a woman? Do we ask if there is a history of involvement with other men? Do we mutually agree to have STD workups when we see that this may potentially go somewhere? Typically, we may ask some of these questions but certainly not all. Why so? Is it because we are afraid of scaring our Prince Charming away? Do we go against logic and convince ourselves that we can "trust" this person and that surely he doesn't have any of these issues? Is it because a man looks "straight" that we dare not fathom the thought of him being one who is also attracted to men? We have a tendency to disregard the possibility of certain things if what we see pleases our eyes. And this is exactly where the enemy is able to come in and trick us up. Satan knows what we like. He knows just how to deceive us into doing what he wants us to do.

So where is God in all of this? More than likely we've left him. He probably didn't move fast enough. Or perhaps in our own reasoning we feel like this is God. That surely Mr. Right has finally arrived. But remember God clearly tells us in his word:

> Be anxious for nothing, but in everything by prayer and supplication, with thanksgiving, let your requests be made known to God; and the peace of God, which surpasses all understanding, will guard your hearts and minds through Christ Jesus.
>
> (Phil 4: 6–7, NKJV)

Often times, we fall head over heels at the mere thought of love and quickly forget everything that the Lord has instructed us to do. We quickly move the other person into our homes and/or within a short period of time engage in sexual relations. We then become convicted and attempt to hide from God. Our prayers often times become shorter and shorter because we feel so guilty. We feel as if we've let God down so we may stop communicating with him altogether. All the while, God is right there attempting to steer us in the right direction. Yet by this time we have become blindsided.

It may feel a bit awkward to drill a potential mate or even someone that you are already involved with or even married to, yet it is so important to be open and honest in a relationship. Real intimacy is only possible to the degree that we can be honest about what we are doing and feeling. When lying or deception begins to dominate a relationship, the relationship begins to deteriorate, and hearts eventually harden. One may sense that there is a lot to lose by telling the truth, and something to be gained by not telling the truth. We must remember lies are at heart deceptions, and over time can and will destroy a relationship. I cannot stress enough the importance of building a relationship on trust. If you cannot trust your partner, or your partner cannot trust you, then there is no foundation for the relationship. Lying about small things eventually leads to lying about larger things. It's only a matter of time before one becomes entangled in a web of lies. Withholding information is still lying.

The good news is you don't have to be an FBI agent to know when you are being deceived. Listen to the loud bells and whistles that are going off in your head and in your heart. If something doesn't feel quite right; it probably isn't. That "gut" feeling is the Holy Spirit attempting to give you a nudge. Please don't ignore the warning signs.

Renee's Story

When the truth finally came out, I had been married to Steve for fifteen years. We'd been blessed with four beautiful children. Steve was a sergeant major in the military and also a deacon in our church. I considered my husband to be a man of strong faith. Yes we had our ups and downs, but all marriages do. For the most part I felt content. It was about seven years ago when I received my first warning. I was doing some spring cleaning and came across a shoe box filled with pictures. The pictures were of my husband cuddled up with some strange woman. As I continued looking, I saw pictures of him holding a newborn. I immediately showed Steve the pictures, and he literally flew off of the handle. He went on this rampage proclaiming that the pictures meant nothing. He claimed that the woman was an old friend from high school and that the newborn was her daughter. He went on and on claiming it to be nothing and instructed me to drop it. He refused to answer any more questions. When I think back to it now, I must've been out of my mind to let that slide. I simply swept it under the rug. I wanted to believe him."

Years went by but I never forgot the pictures. Against my better judgment I decided to just let things be. I convinced myself that I was just being insecure and that it must've been nothing after all. I ignored the unsettled feeling that I would get every time he came up with some last minute excuse for having to come home late or all of sudden needing to go out of town for the weekend. I ignored the fact that he never let me touch his phone and even took it into the bathroom with him. I even ignored the fact the Steve accidentally called me one evening, and I could hear the voice of a little girl calling him "daddy" and lots of laughter. When I began to scream his name, the call dropped. When he made it home that evening, he convinced me that the voice I heard was his friend's child. Now how many friends do you have that would allow their daughter to call another man daddy? I don't know of a single one who would. By this time, I was about to blow a fuse. I knew that my husband was hiding something.

Finally, I was ready for the truth. I decided one evening to do an internet search of my husband's name. Not only did his name show up but also pictures. I clicked on the link and was lead to an online photo album. There were pictures of that same woman along with my husband and a seven-year-old girl. They were celebrating her seventh birthday in Disney World. Steve did not come clean until I showed him the new evidence. He finally confessed to be the father of that child. He admitted to having an affair with this woman for the past eight years.

What do you do when your husband or significant other deceives you in such a manner? Do you just walk away? Do you kick yourself because you ignored the warning signs? Do you not realize that liars lie and cheaters cheat? Nine times out of ten, if he did it once he will do it again. It's only a matter of time. If you are married, it's a choice that you will have to make. There is spiritual counseling and help available if you so choose to save your marriage. But, for those of you who are simply in a relationship, my advice would be to go. He's obviously not ready for a serious commitment. Often times when we find ourselves in situations such as this, we forgive the man and hate the woman. We act as if everything is her fault, and we foolishly convince ourselves that he simply fell victim to her *jezebel* spirit. We want to believe him so badly that we do. We believe that he wasn't thinking or must've been out of his mind. Perhaps we want to believe that things just happened, and now since he's busted he's conveniently done with her? Yeah right. How many times will we fall for these same old lines? Or should I say same old *lies*. There is no sense in being angry with the woman. If it were not her, he still would've had three million other options to choose from. Besides, your commitment was with him. It was he who lived a life of deception and became entangled. What's done in the dark always comes to the light. It's only a matter of time.

> For there is nothing hidden that will not be disclosed, and nothing concealed that will not be known or brought out into the open
>
> (Luke 8:17, NLT)

What happened to Karman and Renee could happen to any of us. This is real life. We empower men to be liars and deceivers. We are far too accepting and far too trusting. Time and again we fail to challenge a lying man even when we sense that something is not right. It's either that or our self-esteem is so low that we convince ourselves that we have too much at stake to simply walk away or show him the door. What we have to realize is that we don't have to accept this type of behavior. A person can only do to you what you allow. Think about it. What will it really take for you to come to your senses? Will it take a situation like Karman? God forbid. When will we as women realize that expecting him to change, or come back home, or realize the error of his ways, or simply "man up" is simply a fantasy that we've created in our own minds out of selfish desires. At some point we have to start using common sense. More likely than not, things will not change, it won't get any better; and those of us who are *patiently waiting* are simply wasting our precious time.

ONE STRIKE, HE'S OUT

> But even when I stop crying, even when we fall asleep, and I'm nestled in his arms, this will leave another scar. No one will see it. No one will know. But it will be there. And eventually all of the scars will have scars, and that's all I'll be—one big scar of a love gone wrong.
>
> —Amanda Grace

I've been alluding to intimate partner violence throughout this entire text. Yet, I would be remiss if I did not dedicate a chapter solely to this topic. For one, this is certainly one of my largest burdens. As you've read, I was victim. What I haven't mentioned is that most if not all of the women in my family have also been victims of this form of violence. My closest friends have all been victims as well as the vast majority of the women who've I've counseled with. We each have come from different walks of life, yet how is it that we share this common trait? Obviously this problem needs to be addressed.

According to the National Center for Victims of Crime, of female murder victims in 2010, 38% were killed by a husband or boyfriend. At some point during their lifetime, approximately 42.4 million women were victims of rape, physical violence, and/or stalking by an intimate partner.

Of female victims, 64% experienced violence by an intimate partner during their lifetimes. Of these women, 57% experienced physical violence alone, and 36% experienced physical violence in combination with another type of violence

A recent study published in the journal *Science* reports that around the world, approximately 30% of women aged fifteen or older have suffered from intimate-partner violence. The rates of reported abuse varied significantly by region. In Sub-Saharan Central Africa, two-thirds of women have been victimized, marking this area the highest portion of those affected by intimate partner violence on the planet. In North America, intimate partner violence typically affects one in five women. However, we must be mindful that not all women feel comfortable self-reporting abuse. Therefore, these numbers could potentially be much higher.

An act of intimate partner violence takes place every twelve to fifteen seconds. Can you remember the last time a week went by without you hearing about a husband, boyfriend, or lover who assaulted or killed his wife or girlfriend? If you decide to call any police precinct, I'm sure that they will tell you that they receive more reports of domestic disputes than anything else. Believe it or not, there are some men who actually believe that they have been privileged by God to abuse women. There are men out there who purposefully lure women into domestic violence nightmares. Since many of us remain unaware of its prevalence, we become prime targets for abuse. For some reason we feel as if we are exempt from it. If we are in an abusive relationship, we feel as if the statistics are incorrect; and that if he promises not to do it again, he won't.

Regardless of what Prince Charming may tell you, the truth is this: if he's abusing you, he doesn't love you. Be it mental, emotional, or verbal—it's all abuse. You should have a zero tolerance level for this. Your rule should be "One strike, he's out." Period. If he hits you once, please believe that he is going to hit you again. He can make every excuse in the world but please get this into your head—it's only a matter of time before it happens again. If you're in a relationship where you are being abused, run. I'm sorry, but I just can't say it any sweeter than that. It doesn't matter if he was drunk, or ticked off about something, lost his job, wasn't thinking, or whatever his excuse of the week may be. Leave him. Pack your suitcase and get the heck out of there. If you have children, pack them up to and don't forget the dog. If you have to creep out while he's at work, do so. Whatever you need to do to save your life, do it. Do not give him any more chances. He will not change.

You must realize that you deserve better. You are to forgive him but that doesn't mean that everything is okay. Let go of the pain, let go of the hurt, let go of the anger. Don't blame yourself. It happened—it's over—and with God's grace move on and don't look back.

Kim's Story

I got married at the age of nineteen to a man I had known for less than a month. Immediately I became pregnant. Within four years, I'd given birth to three daughters. My husband was not a very good husband or father. He was never supportive in any way. He ran the streets while I was at home rocking babies. But, I was young and did not want to raise my girls alone. Even though I felt like I was alone anyway, I held on to the idea of having a husband. So I stayed. In fact I stayed for twelve years before finally realizing that this marriage was broken beyond repair. I just could not hold on any longer. So eventually I left him. I took the children, and we separated. He didn't protest. I felt like I was finally in a place to live and breathe again. Sadly, I was mistaken. I met a man who seemed to be everything that I had been hoping and praying for. We met at a park one evening and almost instantaneously we became joined at the hip. It felt as if I could not breathe without him. He claimed to feel the same way. This was certainly refreshing for me considering I'd already wasted about twelve years with a man who cared not to notice me at all. This guy would bring me flowers "just because." He was such a charmer. He even seemed to get along with my girls who at that time were teenagers and hard to get along with. One warning sign that I chose to ignore however was the fact that he'd just gotten out of prison. I overlooked his past because he always reminded me that he had learned from his mistakes.

He moved in with me and the girls rather quickly, I must admit. But based on my track record, you could say that I love to do things fast. Besides, everything seemed just so perfect. He made breakfast in bed on Saturday mornings. He was neat and for once I didn't have to beg for a man's attention. But gradually things began to change. The abuse did not start out physical it started with cruel words such as "I can do so much better than you." Then he would complain about the house not being clean enough. Then he had problems with my friends. Then he began having issues with the noise level in the house. He said my kids were too loud. The list of complaints seemed to grow by the day. Of course, me being foolish tried to quickly fix whatever he described as broken. Yet, things only got worse. Then the physical abuse started. If we had a spat, he would grab my arm and then quickly apologize. But things quickly worsened. The grabbing turned to punches. Each time I didn't get something right the first time, he would begin to punch me in the head or jaw or eye. Then the punching turned into kicking, cutting, and burning. Yes even burning. I remember taking a hot dish from the oven one evening. He looked at the meal and said it wasn't browned properly. So he grabbed the dish with an oven mit and threw it at me. The food and oils burned the side of my neck and arm. I was hiding all of this from people who loved me because I didn't want to be judged. I felt as if I had no one to turn to. The final straw and the single most horrible thing that changed everything was the day that we went over to a neighbor's house for a cook out. He accused me of flirting with one of the guys there. To be honest, I don't even remember looking at anyone and couldn't even figure out who I supposedly flirted with. He acted as if everything was fine until we made it back home. He began accusing me of being involved with the guy and went for his gun. He put the gun inside of my mouth and cocked it. I remember being so afraid. My heart was beating so fast. He told me that I should be shot in the mouth since I had a lying tongue. I remember praying to God for mercy. I asked God to forgive me for all of my sins. Believe it or not, his uncle showed up out of nowhere and convinced him not to kill me. I grabbed my girls and got as far away from him as I could. I didn't take anything with me. All we had were the clothes on our backs. I knew that I could buy more clothes, but my life could not be replaced.

I share my story not for pity but to point out that you never know how things will end if you chose to hook up with someone who abuses you. I never would've imagined in a million years that I would become one of those women that you read about. If someone had told me that this would someday happen to me, I probably would've laughed. I realize now that it doesn't matter how good you are, or how smart you are, or how pretty you are—this can happen to anyone if you fail to ignore the warning signs. God spared my life, yet there are so many women who are not alive to say the same. I am no longer ashamed of what happened to me. If my testimony will save one person then its worth all of the pain it recreates to tell it.

Any women who is actively dating or seeking a mate must know the warning signs of an abuser. If you are not aware of the warning signs, you will be easy prey. The best scenario is to be aware of the signs before you get into a relationship. Not after you've become trapped. Until you can easily recognize who has abusive tendencies and who does not, you should keep practicing. Do not commit to anyone until you can clearly see who's safe and who's not. As in Kim's story and many of the others throughout this text, the abuse did not start off as physical. Typically the abuser starts with non-verbal cues. He has a problem with all of your friends all of a sudden, or he wants to control your spending, or he begins to nag about every little thing. Perhaps he wants to make all of the decisions without your input or hollers and screams at traffic lights. These are all warning signs, but we tend to excuse these erratic behaviors as temperament issues instead. Then there are those who intentionally ignore warning signs. You are an abuser magnet. You see the person acting inappropriately, yet you completely write it off. I remember long before I became involved with the man who swore he would kill me. I observed him. With my own eyes I witnessed his controlling issues. I saw the way he behaved with his other friends. Most of the people around him were afraid of him. So why in the world did I put myself in such a predicament? That's a question that I have no answer to. I obviously had poor judgment and as a result it almost cost me my life.

Morgan's Story

I moved from Oklahoma to Mississippi to get out of a mentally abusive situation. I was tired of the drama and wanted a fresh start. So I left everything that I loved in a desperate attempt to start my life over. I promised myself that I was going to make better choices from then on when it came to dating and potentially marriage. So for once, I found myself single. Since high school I had been in one serious relationship after the next. Every single one of them had issues too. I finally recognized the pattern and realized that I needed to figure out why I kept picking Mr. Wrong. I wanted to make sure that it didn't happen again. Within a short period of time I began to meet new friends. Yet it didn't take long for me to realize that I was very lonely and desperately needed a man's attention. One day while walking outside of my apartment to the mail box, I met this guy. He looked a little wild, which is normally not my thing. I was typically more into the smooth-charmer type. Yet there was something about the way that he looked at me. It was as if he'd seen an angel. At least this is how he later described it to me. What I realized was that even though he didn't look smooth he was definitely a smooth talker. I agreed to a date after. Next thing you know, he moved in with me. We rarely argued, he bragged on me constantly, and I never saw any signs that he might get violent. But I couldn't figure out where all of his money was going to. He would get paid and the next morning he was broke. I never said anything. I didn't want my nagging to run him away. He hid the drugs at first and then when he realized how laid back I was, he started doing drugs in front of me. This was all new to me. I didn't think smoking marijuana and popping prescription drugs was much of a biggie, so I guess that's why I didn't say anything. Next thing you know, we began to run out of money. My income was not enough to support us both, and it just seemed as if money kept disappearing from our joint account. We ended up losing my apartment and having to move way out to an old family property. Our only neighbor was a long distance away.

We moved together but I finally came to grips with myself and realized that I no longer wanted this relationship. He was too wild and also had a worsening drug problem. I confronted him one morning and told him that I wanted out. He had no reaction. He seemed unconcerned. I noticed that he seemed a little disconnected, but I just figured he was high on pot or something. Later on that evening some of his family was over to the house. I didn't want them to sense anything, so I pretended as if everything was okay. His family wanted beer, so I went out to the store and purchased an eighteen pack. Oddly, his family didn't drink anything. He drank all of them by himself and passed out on the living room floor. His family left and I went on to bed. I laid there thinking about moving plans. I could not wait to get away from this lifestyle. I asked myself how in the world did I get here again. Of course all I could do was cry as my heart filled with regret. Why was I so desperate for love? This isn't even love. I was never attracted to him in the first place so why did I settle? Why did I allow him to do drugs? Why did I agree to pay all of the bills? Am I crazy or something? Before I could answer my own thoughts, he burst into the bedroom. I honestly thought that it was the devil himself. He ran toward me without saying one word and rammed my head into the flat screen TV mounted on the wall. He then began to choke the life out of me. He lifted me up off of the ground and literally threw me across the room. My back shattered a mirror. Pieces of glass got into my skin, eyes, and hair. I was in so much pain. I lay there on the floor and pretended to play dead. I knew that if I even attempted to fight back he was going to kill me for sure. Before I could try to make sense of everything I felt him dragging me by my hair. He threw me down a flight of stairs. I knew for sure every bone in my body was broken. He hurried to where I was and again grabbed my head and ran it through a door. My body was on one side of the door and my head was on the other. He then told me, "You are going to die tonight." I remember begging him to please think about what he was doing. But it seemed to only fuel him more. I knew then that I would never see my mother again. I would never see the daughter again that I left behind to find the "new me." He smashed my head into another wall. By this time I was bleeding profusely and in and out of consciousness. He rammed my head into another wall. Then for some reason he turned his back. I have no idea where I found the strength, but I made a run for it. I dashed out of the door completely naked and began running down the street. I began crying out to God and asking him to please forgive me for my sins. I just knew that at any moment he was going to catch up with me and kill me. As I made a dash for the neighbor's house I saw headlights gleaming down our country road. I began to run faster. It appeared to be my neighbor's pick-up truck. I began screaming, "Help me!" The truck began to come closer, and I began to run even faster. We met in the middle of the road, and my neighbor let me in. We hurried under the garage and within seconds I could hear my abuser banging on its door. I ran in the house of course not knowing my way around. I was so afraid. I stumbled into a bedroom and found his wife there. She looked horrified. She gave me clothes as her husband called the police. Within minutes blue lights were everywhere. They caught him. He had a butcher knife in his hand and had planned to stab me, but I made it to the truck just in time. He went to jail and was later charged with attempted murder. After my release from the hospital, I packed my things and went back home to Oklahoma. I suffered from blunt head trauma, lacerations to my kidneys and spleen, and multiple broken bones. To this day I still have nightmares of that night. I should be dead. If there is anyone out there in an abusive situation, please do what it takes to get out. Please realize that what happened to me can happen to you or worse. It's totally not worth it. You will get over the so-called love. Besides, love does not hurt! Please stop making excuses and run!

I pray that these testimonies have touched your heart. If you can relate in any shape, form, or fashion, I beg of you to recognize the danger of your own situation. If it doesn't apply to you perhaps it applies to someone close to you. Life is too short and precious to lose it over something that you had control over. If you feel trapped in your current situation, I urge you to reach out to family and friends. Don't be ashamed. They will support you. If you feel as if you have no one to reach out to, please contact your local church. They can point you in the right direction. At this point, all that matters is your safety and your sanity. He doesn't love you. Love would never behave in such a manner. The sooner you realize that, the better.

The Word of God clearly defines what love is. If your partner displays behaviors that are inconsistent with what is described below, please rethink your situation.

> Love suffers long and is kind; love does not envy; love does not parade itself, is not puffed up; does not behave rudely, does not seek its own, is not provoked, thinks no evil; does not rejoice in iniquity, but rejoices in the truth; bears all things, believes all things, hopes all things, endures all things.
>
> (1 Corinthians 13:4–8, NKJV)

Jenna's Story

I left my first husband Ricky in the spring of 2005. Over time, our relationship seemed to have dwindled away. He hardly had time for me and was very controlling and jealous. I knew that he had other women, but I put up with it for quite a while. I didn't care as long as at the end of the day he came home to me and the kids. But eventually I got fed up and left. Ricky did not allow me to take the kids with me.

It wasn't long after that I met Mike. We met over the internet and became good friends. We would tell each other anything and everything. He had recently divorced and needed me as much as I needed him. When we first met face-to-face, I was a bit alarmed. He was dressed in leather from head to toe. But I figured his style was that of a typical biker and quickly got over it. He seemed pleasant, very attentive, and always double checked to make sure that I was okay. We immediately moved in together. The first six months with Mike were great. He looked after me well, and I didn't want for anything. I didn't have to lift a finger. But gradually things began to change. I had always been a confident woman. I always dressed in named brand of clothing and never went anywhere without make up. My hair was always perfect, and I made weekly trips to the salon for styling. Well, Mike all of a sudden had a problem with this. He said I looked too trendy and needed to tone down a bit. So I did. I began to wear less makeup, made less frequent trips to the salon, and began to wear baggier clothes. Yet he still wasn't satisfied. I remember us going out to a restaurant once and the waiter asked me for my drink order. He instantly cursed the man out and that night when we got home I got my very first beating. He said he beat me for conversing with the waiter. I was only trying to give the young man my drink order. Within a couple of days he set new ground rules. I could not wear skirts, fitted shirts, or make-up—period. He repeatedly told me that I was absolutely worthless and could not do any better than him.

In the spring of 2006, Mike asked me to marry him and like a fool I said yes. I was not allowed to invite anyone from my family or my children to the wedding. Only his family could be present. On the day that we were getting married, I was miscarrying our first baby. But that didn't stop the day, nothing would. Mike told me to "get over it." The following day I had a scan and was told that I had lost the baby. On our wedding night Mike insisted that we consummate our marriage even though I was cramping badly. He demanded that I take my clothes off. When I refused, he raped me. I slowly learnt just to agree with everything Mike said as it was easier to live that way. According to him, he was always right. About three months later, I became pregnant again. Mike told me that he wanted nothing to do with it. Yet when company was around, he acted as if he was the perfect husband and soon-to-be father. He didn't attend any scans or antenatal appointments. I was still expected to do the entire usual household and woman's jobs, as Mike would call them, even though I was having a hard time with the pregnancy. In the midst of all of this, he would have these bouts of rage. He would punch me in my head or legs and always pull out chunks of my hair.

The day that I went into labor, Mike did not believe me. He made me walk with him five miles and back to make sure that I was in labor. He said he didn't have time to waste sitting up at a hospital if it wasn't time to deliver. I later went to the hospital where they told me after scanning me that the baby had died. He weighed seven pounds and an ounce and was so beautiful. Mike wouldn't even look at him. He said, "I've been there and done that." I guess he meant the fact that his first wife had also lost a child but at the time I didn't know it. He left me to arrange the funeral all by myself. He did not attend. After that, the beatings worsened. I was regularly punched, kicked, and spat at for any little thing. I found out I was pregnant again about six months later. This time I did not tell Mike until I was about four months. At first he seemed happy, but then he accused me of having an affair. He said he wasn't the father. The beatings worsened. Now he was quite comfortable with kicking and punching me in the stomach to go along with the punches in the head and legs.

As a woman I felt worthless and that my only point to life was to be his punching bag. I began to pray daily for someone to come and get me, and I used to phone my friend but as soon as she spoke to me I would make up a story of wedded bliss. I couldn't face telling anyone the truth. I felt as if I were a failure. I was so ashamed. When I went for my first scan with the third pregnancy, I was told that I was carrying a little boy. When I told Mike this, he said, "I hope not. I want another girl. I don't like boys, they are wimps." My pregnancy was very high risk due to the previous complications and the previous baby being stillborn. Mike said so, "So what? You want the little bastard. I could care less." Once again I had to go to all of my doctor visits alone. On my eighth month, I got the beating of all beatings. Mike came home from work drunk. I told him that he shouldn't have driven home that way. As soon as the words came from my mouth, he punched and kicked me so hard that I landed across the room. I somehow got away from him and ran to the neighbors. I went to the emergency room and was told that I had a mild concussion but that the baby was okay. My neighbor called Mike to tell him that I was okay. Still drunk, he came to the hospital just to spit in my face. He then left. The next morning he was full of apologies and of course I forgave him. I had a week's break from the abuse and he actually took me shopping for baby stuff. At 34 weeks I went into full labor. I called the ambulance. Mike actually rode in the ambulance with me. But became angry when he realized we had to go to a hospital further away because of my being high risk. He called me all sorts of names in the ambulance and again spit in my face for the inconvenience. Mike called a ride and left once we made it to the hospital. He said he didn't feel like sitting up there with me. To fast forward, I finally gave birth to our son the next day without Mike's presence. I ended up staying in the hospital for five days but wished I could've stayed there forever.

Upon my return home, I stumbled across Mike's divorce papers. I just had to read them. The only difference between the ex-wife's story and mine was the name. He had also been accused of molesting their two sons. I panicked. I did not want him near my child. Yet I didn't mention it to him and I didn't leave.

The final straw happened when he came in again from work drunk. I was feeding our son. He walked in and began screaming at me. He said I only care about the baby. He snatched the baby from my arms and told me that he was going to kill us both. He ripped the ceiling fan from the ceiling in one swoop and slung it at me. It hit me in the head and blood began spewing. He then began dragging me through the house while punching and kicking me. He dragged me into the bathroom and began forcing my face into the toilet. I knew for sure that my life was over. I could not breathe. I could not see. Everything went black. I felt him tying me up. He dragged me out to the garage and threw me in the trunk. He left the baby in the house alone. I heard the car start and felt it reversing. Within moments we were on the road. He was swerving terribly. I remember praying to God to please help me. I knew that he was probably going to go bury me alive somewhere. Within moments I heard sirens. Mike had been stopped by an officer for driving recklessly. I began banging on the trunk and screaming for help. One of the officers heard me and opened it. By that time they had Mike in the back of the police car. It was obvious that he had been driving under the influence, but he also was covered in my blood. They got me out and all I kept screaming was "My baby!" I didn't know what had happened to him. The police allowed me to call a neighbor who went into the house and found him safe and sound. I never went back to that house. After being released from the hospital, I moved far away. I have not seen Mike since the day he was sentenced for attempted murder and abduction. To anyone who reads this, this can happen to you. If you know that you are in a dangerous situation I urge you to get out of it immediately. Tomorrow may be too late.

FOOLISHLY IN LOVE

> Our wisdom comes from our experience, and our experience comes from our foolishness.
>
> —Sacha Guitry

Let me start the chapter with a recap. Never fall in love with a man who doesn't love you. Never bend over backwards for a man who won't bend for you. Don't go out of the way for a man who won't do the same for you. Don't give your all to someone who gives you nothing. If a man tells you that he doesn't want a commitment, believe him then move on. If a man tells you that you can have everything but his heart, move on. And once again…if your so-called man has a wife—move on! Please! It's so not worth it! Nothing is worth your soul. Not to mention God is not pleased with such behavior. Please stop the madness. I know that I've alluded to this already, but I don't think that it can be emphasized enough. The desire to have another woman's husband is from the pits of hell. You had better recognize it as such. You will get burned. It's foul play.

> For the commandments say, "You must not commit adultery. You must not murder. You must not steal. You must not covet." These—and other such

> commandments—are summed up in this one commandment: "Love your neighbor as yourself."
>
> (Romans 13:9, NLT)

As you read through this chapter, please take some time for self-inventory. No one knows your situation better than you. If you are behaving loosely and foolishly all in the name of "love" or for your own selfish desires to be met, I beg of you to stop it. Okay, now let me drive this home with some real-life scenarios.

Lipstick on the Counter

If your wanna-be man invites you over while the Mrs. or soon-to-be Mrs. is at work, why did you agree? What's the matter with you? Not only are you playing the role of a fool you are risking your very own destiny. The decisions that you make right now can affect you ten years from now. Please think! The last time you snuck in, did you not see her lipstick on the counter and her earrings on the nightstand? Did he even try to hide it? No. So why are you letting him hide you? Aren't you better than that? Do you think God created you to be kept secret? No he did not. Did you not see her clothes in the closet? And yes… that was a picture of her on the nightstand. You can say that you don't mind, and she's the fool and this and that. But let's be real here. You can't possibly enjoy sneaking and creeping around. You can't possibly enjoy being shushed if she calls while you're around. The devil is a liar, and he's been lying to you.

I discussed the topic (why men cheat) with a licensed professional counselor not long ago and this is what he told me. He said men often cheat for the power and control. Of course I immediately asked him to better explain. He then went on to say that back in his cheating days, he wanted to see if other women would react to him in the same way that his main woman did. Okay, hold up. This is not some randomized control trial. Yet we as women often have no problem being in the experimental group. Do you not see that? He wanted to experiment to see if he would receive the same reaction from various women. He went on to say that he never took down his woman's picture from his nightstand. He never put up away of her items.

He then broke it down a bit further by stating that some of the women who came over to his apartment placed that same picture face down. Others placed it inside of the drawer. Some were not bothered one bit and left it as positioned. Now do you expect a man to respect you if you're carrying on like this?

Listen, I've been down this road before. I played this role, and in the end I was the one still lonely and looking foolish. And to answer my own question—of course I was not respected. I received the treatment rightfully deserved. It doesn't matter what lies he's feeding you. ("I'm going to leave her or I'm just there for the kids.") It's all lies. Don't believe it. Nine times out of ten, he is not going anywhere. If he does leave her for you, what type of reward do you expect to get in the end? More than likely he will move on and find a woman who respects herself enough to not have dealings with a person who has stood before God and made vows with someone else in the first place. Or he'll choose a girlfriend who has standards. Good men are not hard to find. The problem is some of us are too busy trying to make someone else's man our man.

The Bible teaches:

> The man who finds a wife finds a treasure, and he receives favor from the LORD.
>
> (Proverbs 18:22, NLT)

It never once said for you to go out searching for him. So let us stop doing that.

Holding it Down

I know of so many women who place their lives on hold while spending their time, gas, money, and efforts on visiting boyfriends in jail. Now listen, I've played this role before too. He told me everything that I wanted to hear as long as I was sending him Vienna sausages and ramen noodles, accepting his collect calls, and putting money on his books. He was so in love as long as I was making those weekly visits to see him. He mailed me letter after letter after letter. I had boxes full of them; yet the moment he smelled free air, he wouldn't even answer my calls or text messages. I'm not trying to be ugly, but the truth is the truth. I remember within two weeks of freedom; he and another woman were hanging out in my household at about four o'clock in the morning while I was working. When I questioned the young lady about what in the world possessed her to come to my house, she told me that she knew nothing about me. He told her that he was a single parent and working hard to support his children. Okay and she bought that lie? I then asked her did she not find it odd that he took her to one of the kid's room to supposedly "watch TV" instead of to his own bedroom? She then gave me a blank stare. Now I do believe that he lied to her. But then there is this thing called common sense. We have to be observant. And why would someone go home with a complete stranger in the first place? We must start thinking. It's far too dangerous. He could've been a killer for all she knew. We cannot keep putting ourselves in these positions. And all for what? What did she think she would gain by spending the night with him? Fleshly fulfillment that's forgotten about by tomorrow that same time? Even if she reminisces... The typical cheating man is on to the next, and the thrill only lasts for so long. Within one year this same man that I placed my life on hold for again went back to jail for longer than I care to mention. Ladies, don't fall for *jail house* talk. If you are married, the situation is different because you vowed to God "until death do us part." But for those of you who call yourselves *holding it down* for a baby daddy or boyfriend, please don't fall for this web of lies. Please wish him good fortune and good health then say good-bye. You deserve so much better. I'm not judging the person on what they may have done to wind up in jail. I'm advising you to take some time and think about this. If the tables were turned, would you get that same dedication and love from him? Probably not. Your relationship probably wasn't that great before he even went to jail. But now that he's there, of course he's going to tell you everything that you want to hear. Of course he's going to say that he's ready to change now. He'll probably ask to marry you too if he hasn't done so already. Please think! Don't fall for this.

Count the Cost

> And what do you benefit if you gain the whole world but lose your own soul?
>
> (Mark 8:36, NLT)

Have you ever heard of any of your girls refer to someone that they are involved with as a "sponsor"? Or perhaps "sugar daddy" or "cake daddy" may be more familiar terms. You might think that this form of dating is all a bit of a joke but in reality this kind of thing happens and a lot more than you would think. I hear women openly speaking on this all the time as if it is acceptable. Keep in mind, typically the "'sponsor" or "sugar daddy" or "cake daddy" is not their main man. She may even have a husband. Yet she has this person "on the side." If she needs something or perhaps wants a pair of designer shoes or a designer handbag, she will call up this person who is typically much older. She makes her request known and within a few hours or so he has made a deposit into her bank account for the desired amount if not more. In exchange, she typically gives him sex and/or company. He, of course, could very well be married or involved with someone as well. What really trips me out is the fact that women involved in these types of practices openly discuss it as if it's normal. I've had women advise me to find myself a "sponsor" in times past and stop spending my own money. I've been told that it's much easier to spend someone else's. Okay, but where do we draw the line? I'm not pointing fingers...but come on now...we have a problem here. I once worked with a lady who told me that she's come to the conclusion that she must have at least two active relationships going at the same time. She just can't get everything that she needs from one person. Ladies, this is pure nonsense. It's dangerous physically, emotionally, and spiritually. It's selfish and deceitful. By doing this, you are basically selling your soul to the devil. Think about it. There are some women who are actually willing to give up their bodies in exchange for purses, or shoes, or maybe even to get someone to pay their bills. I remember my friend dealt with an older guy for this very reason; he paid her bills. She said that she had to sleep with him at least once a week in order for him to fulfill his end of the deal. She referred to him as the "old man." She said during sex with him, she always felt as if she needed to vomit. If that's how it made her feel, how do you think it makes God feel? We take what he has given us for our husbands only to pass it out all over town for shoes, purses, trips to the salon, designer clothes, etc. Do we not realize that God is our provider? He has promised in his Word to supply all of our needs (Phil 4:19). We must learn to count the cost. There is a price for our actions even if it feels as if we are secretly getting away with such. God is omnipresent.

One in a Million

There's one more issue that I at least have to mention before I close out this chapter. I was talking with a good friend one evening about women who have children by men who already have several children by several different women; he married none. My friend was telling me about his best friend who happens to have nine children (four children by one woman, a child by some other woman, a child by some other woman, a set of twins by another woman, and a brand new baby by another woman). He's single, lives with his mother, and doesn't have a job. Some of the children are the exact same age. What can this type of man do for you or the children? Absolutely nothing. I know that we all heard about the guy who made the news for having twenty-two children by fourteen different women. At the time that he made headlines he was being sued for child support. The world finds this entertaining. It was said that he may get a reality TV show and that he would use the money to pay child support. The man went on to brag about being a Romeo and how all of the ladies love him. When questioned about how he ended up with so many children he replied, "I was just young and ambitious, and I love women....Hey, you can't knock no man for loving a woman." Each month, the social services spends $7,500 to support his children. This is not cute; it's a shame. What's even worse is that he had to have cooperation from at least fourteen different women to carry this out. Ladies, are we not wiser than this? Even if some of our situations are not quite this extreme it's still happening every single day. We must wake up.

It doesn't matter if you've found yourself in one or all of the above situations. Perhaps you are involved in something that I failed to mention in this chapter, but you know in your heart that it is wrong. Regardless, you can learn from your experiences and move forward. You are where you are but you certainly don't have to stay there. The first step is confession. We've all sinned and fallen short. We've all been foolish at one time or another. Yet God promises to give anyone who asks of him an abundance of wisdom. Let us make a decision today to ask for it.

A WOMAN'S WORTH

It don't take a whole day to recognize sunshine.

—Common

You are precious. You are smart. You are beautiful. You are strong. You are powerful. You are courageous. You are your creator's finest treasure. You are a gift. You are a rarity. You are worthy of love and affection. You are always enough. You are the most stunning of all of God's creation. You are worth more than you could ever imagine, even more than that designer bag that you carry. You are worth more than the price tag on your most expensive pair of shoes. In the eyes of the Lord you are loved and cherished. Regardless of whether you graduated top of the class or dropped out of school. Whether you look in the mirror and love yourself or despise what you see. Whether you are most popular or no one even knows your name. You are a modern day Esther or Mary or Ruth. You have that same power. You too are a daughter of the most high God. You too have an assignment that will change the world. It's time for you to set the enemy straight. Cancel every lie that he's ever told you. You deserve to be loved by someone who will give their all. You deserve respect. You deserve to be treated as the unique individual that you are. You are something that cannot be found just anywhere. A high price was paid for you. You deserve to be loved by a man who will lay down his life for you. You deserve to be loved by a man who cherishes you. He is to care for your physical, emotional, and spiritual needs. He is to never take you for granted. He is to always be kind and considerate. He is never to become short tempered as a result of your imperfections and weaknesses. He is to treat you with the same regard as God treats you.

You must know and understand God's character. He will not send a man who lies and deceives you. He will not send a man who spits in your face and repeatedly tells you that you are nothing. He will not send a man who has a problem with every single thing that you do. He will not send a man who leaves you to cry yourself to sleep at night. God will not send a man who doesn't have time for you. He will not send a man who is insensitive to your needs. God will not send you someone else's husband. God has so much more for you. He did not say, "It is not good that a woman should be alone." What he said was "It is not good that man should be alone." Your creator knows what's best for you. Yet he cannot fill the position until it is first vacated. You have to release yourself from what the enemy has sent in order to receive your true blessing.

Had I known my worth years ago, my life would've taken a totally different path. Back then I didn't realize who I really was. Instead of allowing God to define me, I accepted Satan's definition. As long as Satan can keep you blind to the truth, he wins. I didn't take the time to search out the scriptures for myself. Had I done so, I would've known better than to tolerate people who treated me contrary to how the Word of God says that I am to be treated. A woman who truly knows and understands her worth is a powerful force. She does not settle. She knows what God has promised her, and she holds on to that promise.

> God is not a man, that He should lie, Nor a son of man, that He should repent.
>
> Has He said, and will He not do? Or has He spoken, and will He not make it good?
>
> (Numbers 23:19, NKJV)

God makes haste to perform his word. He watches over it to make sure that it comes to pass (Jeremiah 1:12). Yet in order for his word to manifest you must first know what it says concerning your situation. Growing up, I vaguely remember hearing about the "Proverbs 31 woman." Yet I didn't realize that this was my God-given example of how I should be regarded by a godly man. Nor did I realize my responsibilities as a woman. I didn't understand who I was created to become. Partly because as humans we are typically a product of our environment, we do what we see. We observe those around us and pattern ourselves after them. But if your situation is anything like mine, there were no positive examples. So then what? I grew up witnessing my mother being physically and emotionally abused by my father. I said I would never accept that kind of treatment from anyone but sure enough the pattern repeated itself in my personal life. I witnessed my grandfather's and father's infidelity. I witnessed the passiveness of the women in my family. They simply accepted the behaviors of their men. I witnessed the struggle my mother experienced when she attempted to take us to church on Sundays. I can still remember my father accusing her of liking the preacher even though my father had never set foot in the church to even see who the preacher was. If he had, he would've known that this was nonsense. I remember witnessing the fear that my mother experienced if we were stuck in traffic and were late getting home. I didn't understand that these issues were deep rooted in my family line and had been passed down for at least four generations. But God knew my struggle. He knew the experiences of my childhood. He also knew that one day I would turn to him and recognize that only he could change my situation. It's time out for excuses. God leaves us many examples of how to be a lady. It is plainly noted in his word. This is why the enemy attempts to fight us so strongly in this area. He wants you to fall asleep as soon as you began to read your Bible. He wants you to be too distracted to discover the truth. He wants to keep you oppressed and depressed. He knows that if you ever seek out the truth, you will be set free.

I now realize that a virtuous woman as described in the Book of Proverbs is not just a cute poem to be read aloud on women's day at your church. The woman described is who God intends for us to model after. This same woman is hidden inside each of us, and it is ultimately our responsibility to find her:

A Virtuous Woman

> A wife of noble character who can find? She is worth far more than rubies. Her husband has full confidence in her and lacks nothing of value. She brings him good, not harm, all the days of her life. She selects wool and flax and works with eager hands. She is like the merchant ships, bringing her food from afar. She gets up while it is still night; she provides food for her family and portions for her female

servants. She considers a field and buys it; out of her earnings she plants a vineyard. She sets about her work vigorously; her arms are strong for her tasks. She sees that her trading is profitable, and her lamp does not go out at night. In her hand she holds the distaff and grasps the spindle with her fingers. She opens her arms to the poor and extends her hands to the needy. When it snows, she has no fear for her household; for all of them are clothed in scarlet. She makes coverings for her bed; she is clothed in fine linen and purple. Her husband is respected at the city gate, where he takes his seat among the elders of the land. She makes linen garments and sells them, and supplies the merchants with sashes. She is clothed with strength and dignity; she can laugh at the days to come. She speaks with wisdom, and faithful instruction is on her tongue. She watches over the affairs of her household and does not eat the bread of idleness. Her children arise and call her blessed; her husband also, and he praises her:

"Many women do noble things, but you surpass them all." Charm is deceptive, and beauty is fleeting; but a woman who fears the Lord is to be praised. Honor her for all that her hands have done, and let her works bring her praise at the city gate.

(Proverbs 31:10–31, NIV)

If you choose to remain blind to the truth, you will remain captive. It's fair game. The devil can continue to play with your mind. He can continue to manipulate you. Your experiences will be the same even if you decide to move on to the next person because it's the same spirit at work.

Next thing you know, your daughters will also be victims of spiritual manipulation. They too will date married men. They too will be abused and disrespected. Your sons will beat their wives. They'll become playboys. Some may even develop unnatural desires. Are you just going to kick back and let that happen? You must recognize who you are and put a stop to this vicious cycle. You must be the change that you want to see. God raises up a deliverer out of every family. That person may very well be you.

It is Satan who wants to not only keep you bound but also the future generations of your family. He wants your seeds to be tied up and confused from birth.

> The thief does not come except to steal, and to kill, and to destroy.
>
> (John 10:10, NKJV)

We say that so casually, but it's time to take it for face value. The devil doesn't care who he has to use. Once you really grasp this, you will no longer be lulled by the sweet lies proceeding from the mouth of your ungodly mate. You will see things as they really are and decide that you no longer have to accept anything less than God's best for you.

You are virtuous. You are morally excellent. You can once again be sexually pure if this has been violated. You are forgiven. You are an overcomer. You are strong in the Lord. You have an attractive personality. Your God-given man will long to be around you. You will not once have to beg him to come home or to spend time with you. He will take joy in doing so because he clearly recognizes that you are a gift from God. His words and his actions will align with the Word of God.

Do you remember what happened to Rebekah in the Bible (Genesis 24)? Rebekah found her husband Isaac by faithfully fulfilling her duties at home. She was not out running the streets or trying to save a dead relationship. She wasn't doing anything extraordinary in order to get a man to notice her true value. As a matter of fact she was busy drawing water from the well. Yet she met an aged man there who led her to her husband Isaac. Case in point, if you will get busy about your father's business I guarantee you that he will get busy about yours.

If you desire a man who is not full of empty promises, it's time for you to get on your knees and seek God. Ask God to show you who you really are and what you truly deserve. God will show up if you ask him to. God will never lie to you. God will never treat you as if you were nothing. God places high esteem on the woman. We are supposed to be man's helpmeet not doormat. If a man cannot see what you bring to the table, that's his loss not yours. Stop thinking that you have to convince someone that you are special. He should be able to see that for himself. But in order for him to see it, you must conduct yourself as the woman of God you were created to be. If he doesn't recognize what you are carrying please move on.

My prayer today is for you to begin to see yourself as God sees you. Take all of the energy you've been using to chase after Mr. Wrong and chase after God instead. You will not be disappointed. He will place you back on the potter's wheel and make sure that this time everything is good. He will develop your character. Character is doing what is right, regardless of the consequences. You cannot lose with God.

LETTING GO

> Letting go has never been easy, but holding on can be as difficult. Yet strength is measured not by holding on, but by letting go.
>
> —Len Santos

I wish there was some magic remedy that I could suggest to you that would make all of your troubles quickly fade away. I wish that I could somehow comfort you by saying that it's easy to say "you're not the one" and simply walk away. But unfortunately it's not that simple. If it were, many of us would've left at the first signs of trouble. We wouldn't have lost ourselves in hopes of getting someone to recognize our value. We wouldn't have put up with the abuse. For some, we never would've accepted the outside child or mistress or both. In other cases, we never would've agreed to be the mistress in hopes that he would someday leave her. We wouldn't have involved children. We wouldn't have risked our finances. We wouldn't have jeopardized our credit. We wouldn't have compromised our walk with the Lord. We wouldn't have turned our back to those who were only trying to help us see the real picture. The truth of the matter is; had you known then what you know now you probably would've never given him the time of day in the first place. But now what? How do you move on? You can see that the relationship is clearly not going in the direction that you'd hoped or it's obvious that his interests are elsewhere. You've come to a place where you really are sick and tired of being sick and tired. Yet for some reason you simply can't walk away. Perhaps you don't feel as if you are strong enough. Maybe you feel as if you can't support yourself. It could be that you lack the courage. Perhaps you are afraid of facing the world alone. Whatever the reason, know that you *can* do this. You are more than a conqueror.

By now all of your friends probably think that you're crazy. They have probably offered you all sorts of advice. Yet many of them may be in worse predicaments than you are. Nevertheless, they don't want to hear you say a single word about *him* or the *relationship*. Yet you really do want out. You've realized that enough is enough. But your heart won't let go of the hope that he will somehow change and things can be as you've imagined them to be. I'm going to be quite frank with you. It's time for you to wake up and smell the roses. Start looking at the person not as you want them to be but as they truly are. Unfortunately we do not live in a fairy tale world. Everything does not go according to our plans. But, I can promise you one thing. God has a far better plan.

> For I know the plans I have for you," says the LORD. "They are plans for good and not for disaster, to give you a future and a hope.
>
> (Jeremiah 29:11, NLT)

If someone has lied or deceived you, mistreated you, or no longer has feelings for you; you must recognize that this is not a healthy relationship for you. Yes you may feel a sense of betrayal but it's high time to accept it and move on. What else can you do? It's time for you to get your life back. It's time for you to find you. Moving on does not mean that you can no longer love this person. You can wish them well and hope that they find happiness. However, you must do better for yourself.

As long as we are in bondage, we are not free to do the work and will of the Lord. Satan has us exactly where he wants us. Why do you think that the enemy has so much interest in your relationship in the first place? It's because there is so much power in agreement—a power that he cannot destroy.

> I also tell you this: If two of you agree here on earth concerning anything you ask, my Father in heaven will do it for you.
>
> (Matthew 18:19, NLT)

Listen, whether you care to believe it or not there is an adversary among us. He will do anything and everything to make sure that your destiny is aborted. And guess what? He will do so by any means necessary. He will use the very person that you feel as if you cannot live without to destroy you. He wants to keep your self-esteem low. He wants you to feel worthless. He wants you to feel totally dependent on a man who could care less about you. He never intended for you to discover your true worth. He wants you to believe that you can't get anyone better than the garbage that he sent you. He doesn't want you to walk away. He wants you to believe that things will change if you just hold on. Yet the longer you hold on the more entangled you will become. Even though it's difficult to see past your pain, you must know that God is the ultimate mender of broken hearts. You must try him for yourself.

Terri's Story

God is amazing. He loves us so much that even when we are in the midst of living in sin, he still stands ready and willing to help those who ask it of him. Even if we are not born again, when we call, he will answer. At least that is my story. I remember living with my children's father back in 1995. I first got with him in 1994. Shortly after, I moved in with him and his mother. What a *big* mistake that was. Looking back, I was obviously out of my mind. I don't know what was worse: me living with him, or me living with him and his mother. I've since forgiven them both, had I not I would still have a whole bunch to say about each of them. When I moved in, I was already pregnant with our daughter. It was me, my children's father, his mother, her husband and his sister. My children's father received a disability check of $450 a month. His mother got a check every month for a little over $100. No one else in the house had any form of income. I worked at a local fast food restaurant until he made me quit because I came home three minutes late one time. My parents lived a short distance away. Had I known what I was getting myself into, I could've just stayed home. At least at home, I could eat a decent meal. With my children's father's family, there were days that we didn't have anything at all to eat. Sometimes I would go two or three days with nothing. Other times I was given nothing but bread crumbs and scraps, etc. Remember, I was carrying my daughter at this time. Thoughts of leaving never crossed my mind. I was so messed up in the head. He promised me that things would get better; foolishly I believed him. But things only got worse. He began to verbally and physically abuse me. He would always tell me that I am nothing and that no one else would want me or my baby. He would call me ugly, stupid, skinny, you name it. One time during one of his rampages, he pushed me off of the front porch, and I landed face and belly first on the concrete. I thought for sure that I would miscarry, but I didn't. God obviously has a plan for my daughter.

Eventually, I had the baby and we moved into a low-income apartment. Drug dealers hung out on the corner right by my door. People hung out all times of the night. It was a very dangerous atmosphere. By this time, he had gotten so bold that he would even bring other women home right in front of me and take them to our bedroom. I would become sick to my stomach. I was too afraid to say anything and didn't know how to leave. Sometimes he would even make me watch what he did to them. Back at his mother's house, the abuse was more mental and emotional. In the apartment, it became really physical. He was so violent. I never knew when my next black eye would come or my next emergency room visit. Each time I told the triage nurse at the hospital "I fell." After about fifteen visits, I'm sure that those people didn't believe a word that I said. I still remember the worse beating as if it were yesterday. It came after he had flunked out of pharmacy tech school. He asked me why I thought he failed. I told him (as meekly as I could), "It's because you didn't study." While I had my five-day-old son in my arms, (yes I got pregnant again) he took off his belt and began beating me. The buckle part kept hitting my head and eye. Then while still holding the baby in my arms, he choked me until the vessels in my eyes ruptured. I remember everything going black. I began to lose consciousness. I could see my life flashing before me. It takes the power of God to forgive. I had heard about a man named Jesus. I had heard about how he could deliver you if you really asked. But I wasn't sure if it was true. I honestly didn't even know how to pray. I wasn't sure of how to even begin a conversation with a God, but in my mind I remember saying, "God, if you will spare my life and get me out of this, I promise to never ever go back." Instantly, and I mean instantly, my abuser let me go. My body fell to the couch. Believe it or not my baby was still in my arms unharmed. My husband left the apartment. I called the police and pressed charges on him for domestic violence. They jailed him for a few days. While he was away, I filed a restraining order, packed up my things, and went home to my parents. I enrolled in school. Within a month, my life had already turned completely around. My husband never came after me. I owe my deliverance to God. He was with me during a time that I needed him most and is still with me today. Don't be afraid to let go. If you are willing to take the first step God will make the provisions to safely rescue you, even if you are not in an abusive situation. Maybe you are simply dating someone who is not as committed as you are. Please know that there is better for you. Please walk away. I beg of you.

I realize that there are a lot of relationship materials out there. I'm sure that you can search "How to survive after a break up" or "How to get your man back" in order to get some kind of worldly guidance. But the only true way out is to seek God. This is the very same way that Terri received her deliverance. In her desperation, she cried out to a God that she'd only heard about. Yet, he still answered.

In like manner, this is the way that I received my deliverance. I cried out to God, and he set me free. I could not do it in my own strength. After going through the same scenario over and over and over again, I realized that the problem had to be much deeper than what it appeared to be on the surface. I was entrapped in a viscous cycle of failure. I had become blinded to the truth about who I really was and what I really deserved. It was not until I became down right fed up with the way my life was going and decided to try God that things began to turn around for me. Yes I had been going to church for a long time. I sang in the choir and did all kinds of things for the ministry. You see the enemy doesn't mind you attending church as long as there is no deliverance. But there's a difference between attending church and truly walking with God. It's not just what you do on Sundays and Wednesdays that count. It's what you do when you're all alone. It's those times when no one else can see but God. I was so tired and realized that if I didn't turn to my savior I was going to wind up in a mental institution or worse. So I gave up and decided to go all the way. And sure enough just as he promised in his word, his spirit began to guide me into truth. It was through much fasting and prayer that God began to reveal my real issues. I'm not just saying this based on something that I heard from a friend or from a good sermon. I am telling you what I know to be true from my own experience. God is faithful. When you get real with him, I guarantee you that he will get real with you. When you draw near to him, he will draw near to you. The Lord revealed the roots of my problems to me and will do the same for you. You must put your faith and trust in the true lover of your soul, Jesus Christ. He has your back.

Do you remember what happened to the woman who had been afflicted for eighteen years in the Bible? Let's take a look at it:

> One Sabbath day as Jesus was teaching in a synagogue, he saw a woman who had been crippled by an evil spirit. She had been bent double for eighteen years and was unable to stand up straight. When Jesus saw her, he called her over and said, "Dear woman, you are healed of your sickness! "Then he touched her, and instantly she could stand straight. How she praised God!
>
> But the leader in charge of the synagogue was indignant that Jesus had healed her on the Sabbath day. "There are six days of the week for working," he said to the crowd. "Come on those days to be healed, not on the Sabbath."
>
> But the Lord replied, "You hypocrites! Each of you works on the Sabbath day! Don't you untie your ox or your donkey from its stall on the Sabbath and lead it out for water? This dear woman, a daughter of Abraham, has been held in bondage by Satan for eighteen years. Isn't it right that she be released, even on the Sabbath?"
>
> (Luke 13:10–16, NLT)

Did you catch that? She had been crippled by an evil spirit. As a result she had been suffering for eighteen long years. When Jesus saw her, he called her over and instantly healed her. Are you ready for your healing? Aren't you tired of being burdened down?

> For my yoke is easy to bear, and the burden I give you is light.
>
> (Matthew 11:30, NLT)

Barbara's Story

I finally gathered up the courage to take my three children and get away from the man who beat us on the daily basis, my boyfriend William. I had no family to turn to and no friends. William kept me so isolated that eventually I lost contact with everybody. I had no choice but to go to an emergency shelter. I stayed there with my children for about six weeks. It was very hard. I had no money and no transportation. During this time, William continued to make contact with me. He called me and texted me all day every day. He repeatedly told me how much he loved me and how he was ready to change. He told me that I was his best friend and that he absolutely could not live without me. He apologized for the harm he'd done to me and the kids. He asked me to please marry him and that he would like for us to find a local church. So stupidly I returned home. Things went well for about two weeks. Then the abuse started again. I remember the horrible day as if it were just yesterday. I left the children with William for about forty-five minutes while I headed out to the store to get some things to finish cooking dinner. When I returned, I found our youngest child limp, lying across our bed. I knew that he was dead. His eyes were rolled back in his head and his face was blue. I began to scream and cry as I cradled our lifeless child in my arms. He was bruised from the tips of his fingers to the soles of his feet. He also had bite marks on his cheek and under his chin. I was later told that he had lacerations to his rectum, liver, and intestines. How could I have let things get to this point? How could I have let him sweet talk me back into a situation that resulted in my very own child losing his life. Why could it not have been me instead if someone had to die?

I was charged with failure to protect my child and have fifteen years to serve in prison. William was charged with murder and was sentenced to thirty years without parole. When asked why didn't I leave, all I can say is that I was afraid. He threatened to kill me if I ever left again. I feel so guilty. I only have myself to blame. If you see that your life or the life of your children are in danger. Please let go. You never know when the person who claims to love you so much will actually go beyond the point of no return. It's not worth it.

Barbara left, but she came back unknowingly to a death trap. As difficult as it may seem, if you can clearly see that your relationship is dangerous and or fruitless please ask God for the courage to leave and never turn back. It's not worth your life, the life of your children, or your sanity. I urge you to look to the hills for which cometh your help (Psalm 121:1). Do you not know that all of your help comes from God? There is nothing too difficult for him. He specializes in the impossible. This is not the way your story has to end. You can find peace, joy, and happiness without the person that hurt you. Perhaps he decided to walk away from you. Let me assure you that you can find contentment without him ever coming back. Consider it a painful lesson learned. God can make you brand new. You can look back on your situation and know that it was only God who brought you out.

I thank God for every man who ever hurt me. I thank God for every disappointment. Experience truly is an excellent teacher. My experiences taught me what not to accept. I can now recognize what love really is and what it isn't. I realize now that I settled because I had no idea of my true identity. I was seeking love when I didn't even know how to love myself. I didn't realize that a man who lacks an authentic relationship with God could never have an authentic relationship with me. I was expecting to receive something that simply could not be given. Satan knew all along what I had the potential to become, just as he knows your potential. The longer he can keep you sidetracked, the better for him. This is why the enemy tried so desperately to take me out physically or at least have my mind. He wanted me to keep my mouth shut and not help others get free. He knew that if I ever got serious with God, his trifling tactics would be exposed. Can you make that same commitment? Aren't you ready to shame the devil? There are women in line waiting to be free. Your story may very well be what gives their heart the conviction needed to take that first big step. Your life, struggle, and deliverance is more than just a pebble being dropped into the ocean. You have an assignment. There is work to be done. There may very well be a platform waiting for you. I could be reading your book next. If you will just let Go and let God. Pull yourself up by your boot straps and make a decision to release what you have in your hand in order to receive what God has in his. Remember, weeping may endure for a night, but joy always comes in the morning (Psalm 30). Every storm cloud eventually runs out of rain. Your life is not over. You don't have to be angry, and there is no need for resentment. It had to go this way. It was my failures that actually led me to develop an intimate relationship with Christ. So if it takes you going through what you've gone through in order for the Glory of God to be revealed in your life then so be it. May God give you strength and revelation.

I urge you to taste and see that the Lord is good; you will be blessed for taking refuge in him (Psalm 34:8). You don't have to be a super saint to be healed, delivered, and set free. All you have to do is call on him right where you are. He is your strong tower (Psalm 61:3). He is your shield, your glory, and the lifter of your head (Psalm 3:3). He'll pick you up out of the miry clay and place your feet on a solid foundation (Psalm 40:2). He will restore everything that was lost in due season.

> And I will restore to you the years that the locust hath eaten, the cankerworm, and the caterpiller, and the palmerworm.
>
> (Joel 2: 25, KJV)

He'll steer you safely from the storm. You can do this! Your best days begin right now! Ask God to give you the ability to let it all go. In Jesus' name. *Amen.*

LETTER TO THE READER

I have now fulfilled the mandate given to me by God in regard to the writing of this work. Now the Lord is placing one upon you. You must share this message. Every woman within your circle of influence must get her hands on a copy of this book. We must continuously and relentlessly expose the chaos. There is a sense of urgency in the spirit realm that mustn't be ignored. You will be blessed for your act of obedience.

Blessings to you,
Kellie Lane

LIST OF WEBSITES

Definition of chaos

https://www. google. com/#q=definition+of+chaos

Introduction

http://www. goodreads. com/author/
quotes/4491185. Steve_Maraboli

Heart Disease

http://www. cdc. gov/heartdisease/about.htm

How does heart disease affect women?

http://www. nhlbi. nih. gov/health/
health-topics/topics/hdw/

Quality control

http://www. aleanjourney. com/2013/06/lean-
quote-quality-is-never-accident-it. html

Boundaries

http://www. goodreads. com/
quotes/24553-no-is-a-complete-sentence

Empty Bed

http://www. goodreads. com/quotes/66625-
when-i-get-lonely-these-days-i-think-so-be

Chameleon

http://www. goodreads. com/author/
quotes/3161921. Amanda_Grace

The Deceiver

http://www. goodreads. com/quotes/463916-just-
because-something-isn-t-a-lie-does-not-mean-that

One strike, He's Out

http://quotations. about. com/od/lovequotes/
a/I-Love-Him-Quotes. htm

http://www. victimsofcrime. org/library/
crime-information-and-statistics/
intimate-partner-violence

Foolishly in love

http://www. goodreads. com/quotes/268440-our-wisdom-comes-from-our-experience-and-our-experience-comes

http://www. eurweb. com/2013/07/man-with-22-kids-by-14-different-women-could-get-reality-show

A Woman's Worth

http://songmeanings. com/songs/view/69776/

Letting Go

http://boardofwisdom. com/togo/Quotes/ShowQuote?msgid=251583#. Uu_5brSwWss

CPSIA information can be obtained
at www.ICGtesting.com
Printed in the USA
BVOW00s2148231016
465620BV00035B/151/P

9 781634 1810